MAGIC STORIES

by

Enid Blyton

Containing

The Goblin Aeroplane and Other Stories
The Little Green Imp and Other Stories
&
Run-About's Holiday

D1150368

A Red Fox Book
Published by Random House Children's Books
20 Vauxhall Bridge Road, London SW1V 2SA

A division of Random House UK Ltd

London Melbourne Sydney Auckland
Johannesburg and agencies throughout the world

The Goblin Aeroplane first published by Pitkin 1949, 1951
Red Fox edition 1990
© Darrell Waters Ltd 1949, 1951

The Little Green Imp first published in Mr Icy-Cold,
Enid Blyton's Annual and The Grandpa Clock
Beaver edition 1984
© Text of compilation Darrell Waters Ltd 1984
© Illustrations Century Hutchinson 1984

Run-About's Holiday first published by Lutterworth Press 1951
Sparrow edition 1981, Beaver edition 1988
© Text Enid Blyton 1951
© Illustrations Century Hutchinson 1951

Red Fox compilation 1993

The Enid Blyton signature is the registered trademark of
Darrell Waters Ltd.

Red Fox compilation 1993

This book is sold subject to the condition that it shall not,
by way of trade or otherwise, be lent, resold, hired out, or
otherwise circulated without the publisher's prior consent
in any form of binding or cover other than that in which it
is published and without a similar condition including this
condition being imposed on the subsequent purchaser

Printed and bound in Great Britain by
Cox & Wyman Ltd, Reading, Berkshire

RANDOM HOUSE UK Limited Reg. No. 954009

ISBN 0 09 922801 7

Enid Blyton's

THE GOBLIN AEROPLANE
and other stories

RED FOX

Contents

The
Goblin Aeroplane

'IT'S such a lovely day you can take your lesson books on to the hillside, if you like,' said Mummy one morning to Jill and Robert.

So out they went.

'What have you got to do?' Robert asked Jill.

'I've got to learn how to spell six words,' said Jill. 'They're rather hard. Here they are: mushroom, toadstool, honey, dewdrop, magic and enchantment. Don't you think they are hard, Robert?'

'Yes,' said Robert. 'I'm sure I don't know how to spell them. I've got to learn my seven times table.'

'I'm only up to five times,' said Jill. 'Ooh, isn't it lovely out on the hillside, Robert!'

The two children sat down and opened their books – but it was hard to work. First a lovely peacock butterfly flew by. Then a tiny copper beetle with a shining back ran over Jill's book. Then a robin came and sat so near to them that they hardly dared to move in case he was frightened away.

'I say, Jill!' said Robert at last. 'How much work have you done?'

'None!' said Jill. 'Have you learnt your table, Robert?'

'Only as far as seven times two,' answered Robert. 'It's a pity to have to do homework when the sun is shining so brightly and we'd like to play.'

'Well, let's not do it,' said Jill. 'No one will know, because we can take our books to bed with us tonight, and after Mummy has gone we can get them out and learn our words and our tables then!'

'Oh, no, Jill!' said Robert, shocked. 'Mummy trusted us to do our lessons here, and we must. It would be mean to play when she sent us out here for a treat.'

'All right,' said Jill. 'It would be mean – so let's get on quickly and finish them, Robert.'

The two children turned their backs on one another, put their fingers in their ears and began to learn their spelling and table. They didn't look up once even when the robin flew down at their feet. They meant to do their lessons really properly.

Soon Jill sat up.

'I've finished, Robert!' she said. 'Hear my spelling, will you?'

'Yes, if you'll hear my seven times table,' said Robert. They passed each other their books, and Jill was just beginning to spell 'Mushroom' when a very strange thing happened.

They saw a tiny speck in the sky, which rapidly grew larger. It was bright red and yellow.

'It's an aeroplane, Jill!' said Robert. 'But what a funny one!'

It certainly was odd, for instead of having flat wings like an ordinary aeroplane, it had curved

9

wings like a bird, and it flapped these slowly up and down as it flew.

'It's coming down!' said Jill, in excitement. 'Ooh, look, Robert, it's coming down quite near us!'

Sure enough the strange aeroplane flew swiftly towards them, flapping its odd red and yellow wings. From the cockpit a funny little man peeped out. He waved his hand to them.

The aeroplane suddenly dipped downwards, and with a whirr of wings that sounded rather like a giant bee buzzing, it landed on the hillside near the excited children. They ran up to it in astonishment.

'What a tiny aeroplane!' cried Robert. 'I've never seen one like that before!'

'It's a goblin aeroplane!' said the pilot inside, peeping at them and grinning widely. 'It belongs to me.'

'Are you a goblin then?' asked Jill, in surprise.

'Of course,' said the strange pilot, and he jumped out of his 'plane. Then the children saw that he really was a goblin. His ears were pointed and stuck out above his cap. His body was round and fat, and his feet were as pointed as his ears.

'I've come to ask if you can tell me where Greenfield Farm is,' he said.

'Oh yes,' said Robert. 'It's over that field, then through a path in the wood, then over a stile, then down by the stream, then over the little hill, then–'

'Goodness!' cried the goblin, 'I shall never find it in my aeroplane! Can't you tell me how to get to it from the air?'

'I might, if I were in your aeroplane with you,' said Robert, doubtfully. 'I think I should know what the farm looks like, but I couldn't quite tell you now how to go. You see, I've never been in an aeroplane.'

'Well come for a ride in mine,' said the goblin, grinning. 'You and your sister can both come, and as soon as you show me Greenfield Farm and I land there, you can hop out and run home again.'

'Ooh!' shouted both children in excitement, and they danced up and down in glee. 'Do you really mean it?'

'Of course,' said the goblin. 'Come on, hop in.'

So they climbed into the aeroplane, and the goblin climbed in too. Jill and Robert looked to see how he flew it. It was a very strange aeroplane, there was no doubt of that. In front of the goblin's seat were dozens of little buttons, each with something printed on. One had 'Down' on, one had 'Up', and another had 'Sideways'. Still another had 'Home' on, and a fifth had 'Fast', and a sixth one 'Slow'. There were many more besides.

The goblin pressed the button marked 'Up' and the aeroplane began to flap its strange wings. It rose from the ground, and the children clutched the sides in excitement, for it was a very odd feeling to be in something that flapped its wings and flew into the air.

'There's the farm!' cried Robert, and he pointed to a pretty farm house over to the east. At once the goblin pressed a button marked 'East', and the aeroplane flapped its way to the right. Soon it was over the farm, but to the children's great surprise it didn't land, but flew straight on.

'Aren't you going to land?' asked Jill. 'You've passed right over the farm.'

'Ha ha!' laughed the goblin, and it was such a nasty laugh that the children looked at him in surprise.

'Why don't you land?' asked Robert. 'I don't want to go too far, you know, because of getting home again.'

'You're going to come with me!' said the

goblin. 'You didn't suppose I really wanted to go to the farm, did you? Why that was only a trick to get you both into my aeroplane!'

The children sat silent for a minute, they were so surprised. Jill felt frightened.

'What do you want us for?' asked Robert at last.

'To sell to Big-One the giant,' said the goblin. 'He's lonely in his castle and he wants two children to talk to.'

'But, good gracious, you can't do a thing like that!' cried Robert, in a rage. 'Take us back home at once, or I'll make you very sorry for yourself!'

The goblin smiled a wide smile, and said nothing. Robert wondered what to do. He did not dare to hit the goblin, for he was afraid that the aeroplane might fall. So he just sat there frowning, holding Jill's hand tightly, for he saw that she was frightened.

After about twenty minutes Robert looked over the side of the aeroplane. Far below was a strange-looking country with palaces gleaming on hills, and castles towering high.

'It must be Fairyland,' whispered Jill when Robert pointed it out to her. 'Oh, Robert, this is a great adventure, even if that old goblin is taking us to a giant!'

Just then the aeroplane plunged downwards, for the goblin had pressed the button marked 'Down'. It flew to a great castle standing on a mountain top, and landed on one of the towers. The goblin leapt out and ran to a staircase leading down from the roof.

'Hey, Big-One!' he called. 'Here are two children for you! Where's that sack of gold you promised me?'

Robert and Jill heard great footsteps coming up the stairs, and a giant's head peeped out on to the roof. He had a huge shock of hair, a turned-up nose, a wide mouth and very nice blue eyes as big as dinner plates. The children liked the look of him much better than they liked the goblin.

'So these are the children,' said the giant, in a loud booming voice. 'Well, they look all right, goblin. You can have your sack of gold tonight. I haven't any by me at the moment. Come for it at six o'clock.'

'All right,' said the goblin, and he went back to the aeroplane.

'Climb out,' he ordered, and Robert and Jill climbed down from the cockpit, feeling very

14

strange. The goblin leapt into his seat, pressed the button marked 'Up' and disappeared into the sky, shouting that he would be back that night at six o'clock for his sack of gold without fail.

The giant looked at the two children.

'Will you come down into my kitchen?' he said, in a kind voice. 'I am sure you want something to eat and drink after your ride.'

Robert and Jill felt glad to hear him speak so politely. He couldn't be very fierce, they thought. They followed him down the enormous stairs and came to a vast kitchen where a huge kettle boiled loudly on a great fire.

'Sit down,' said Big-One, and he pointed to two chairs. But neither Robert nor Jill could climb on to the seats, for they were so high up. So the giant gently lifted them up, and then took the boiling kettle from the stove.

He made some cocoa in three great china cups, and set out three enormous plates, on each of which he had placed a very large slice of currant cake.

'Please join me in a little lunch,' he said. 'It is really very kind of you to take pity on me and come to live with me. I didn't think any children would be willing to come here, you know.'

'Why, we weren't willing!' said Robert, in astonishment. 'The goblin got us here by a trick. We didn't want to come here at all!'

'What!' cried the giant, upsetting his cocoa in his surprise. 'Do you mean to say that nasty little goblin brought you here against your will?'

'Yes,' said Robert, and he told Big-One all about the morning's happenings.

Jill listened and nodded her head, eating her currant cake, which was really most delicious.

The giant was terribly upset when he heard about the trick that the goblin had played on the children.

'I don't know what to do!' he said, and two big tears stood in his saucer-eyes. 'I wouldn't have had such a thing happen for the world! Now, however can I get you back again? And oh, dear me, that nasty goblin will be coming for his sack of gold too, and I haven't any. You see, I thought you'd be able to help me with my spells, for children are very clever, much cleverer than stupid giants like me. I thought I'd get you to help me with a gold-spell, and make some gold before the evening.'

'Well, we don't mind helping you a bit,' said Robert, who liked the big giant very much.

'Don't cry. You've splashed a tear into your cocoa, and it will make it taste salty.'

'Will you really help me!' cried Big-One. 'Oh, you good, kind children! Well, I'll just clear away these things and then we'll set about making a gold-spell.'

He put the cups and plates into a huge sink and washed them up. Then he took the children into a big bare room with many chalk circles drawn on the floor. A big pot hung over a fire that burnt with strange green flames.

'Now first of all I've got to write six words in the biggest of these chalk circles,' he said. 'But, oh dear me, I don't know how to spell them! Still, children are very clever, so I do hope you'll be able to help me. Can either of you spell Mushroom?'

'I can!' cried Jill, excitedly. 'I learnt it this very morning! M-U-S-H-R-O-O-M!'

The giant carefully wrote it down in the circle as Jill spelt it. Then he looked up at her.

'Now could you spell Magic?' he asked.

'Yes!' said Jill, 'M-A-G-I-C! That was one of the words I had to learn this morning, too!'

Well, would you believe it, all the words that the giant needed for his spells were the very ones Jill had to learn! Wasn't it a good thing she

had done them so well? The last one the giant wanted was Enchantment.

'That's the hardest one,' said Jill, and she frowned. 'Oh, I do hope I remember it properly. Let me see – E-N–'

'Where's your spelling book, Jill?' asked Robert, terribly afraid that Jill might spell the word wrong after all. 'You could look it up before you spell it.'

'We left both our books on the hillside!' said Jill. 'No, I must try and spell it out of my head. Let me think for a minute – yes, I think I've got it. E-N-C-H-A-N-T-M-E-N-T!'

Big-One wrote it carefully down. Then he drew a toadstool and a mushroom right in the very middle of the circle, put a spot of honey on each, and shook a dewdrop from a piece of grass on to the honey.

'That's all ready for the spell now!' he said. 'What a good thing you knew how to spell Mushroom, Toadstool, Honey, Dewdrop, Magic and Enchantment, Jill. But oh, dear me – the next thing we have to do is very hard!'

'What's that?' asked Robert.

'Well, two of us have to dance round the circle holding hands,' said the giant, 'whilst one stands in the middle chanting the seven times table. But I don't know the seven times table. I only know twice times.'

'I don't know it either,' said Jill.

'But I do!' cried Robert. 'I learnt it this very morning. I can say it! I'll be the one to stand in the middle.'

'Oh, good!' said Big-One, and he rubbed his great hands together in delight. 'Now listen – Jill and I will dance round together, and you must stand still in the middle saying your seven times table at the top of your voice. At the end of it I have to say twelve very magic words, and then, if we've done the spell right, a sack of gold appears right in the middle of the circle!'

'Come on, let's do it!' cried Jill. 'Are you sure you know all your seven times perfectly, Robert? It might spoil the spell if you got something wrong.'

'I'm not quite sure of seven times twelve,' said Robert. 'I think it's eighty-four, but just wait a minute and I'll work it out to make sure.'

He took a piece of the giant's chalk and wrote the figure 12 seven times on the floor. Then he added them up, and sure enough, it made eighty-four, so he was quite right.

Then they started the spell. Jill and the giant danced round the circle, and Robert stood in the middle saying his seven times table at the top of his voice. When he had finished the giant shouted out a string of curious magic words, and all the words he had written inside the ring suddenly vanished!

Then crash! A great sack suddenly appeared in the middle of the circle and knocked Robert down. He was up in a minute, and peeped into the mouth of the sack.

'Yes, the spell has worked!' he cried. 'It's full of gold! Ooh, what powerful magic! And what a mercy I knew my seven times table properly!'

The giant was so pleased. He could hardly thank Robert and Jill enough.

'You don't know how grateful I am to you,' he said. 'I can pay that horrid goblin now, though I don't think he deserves a penny, because he brought you here by a trick. But the next thing is – how am I going to get you home again?'

'I don't know,' said Robert. 'Could you use magic, do you think?'

'No,' said Big-One. 'I don't know any that would take you home. Wait a minute – let me think.'

He sat down on a stool and frowned for five

minutes. Then he jumped up and clapped his hands so loudly that it quite frightened Jill.

'I've a fine plan!' he said. 'The goblin will come in his aeroplane tonight at six o'clock. Now listen – I'll hide you behind a chimney pot on the roof of the castle. When the goblin arrives I'll call him downstairs to the cellar to fetch his gold. As soon as he's gone down the stairs you must pop out, jump into the aeroplane and fly home!'

'But we don't know how to fly a goblin aeroplane!' said Robert.

'Oh, it's quite easy,' said Big-One. 'Didn't you see all those buttons? Well, you just press the one that says 'Up' and then the one that says 'Home', and then the one that says 'Down' when you see your home, and there you are!'

'Well, I think I could do that,' said Robert. 'Anyway, I'll try. But what shall we do till six o'clock?'

'Perhaps you'd like to come out with me in my yellow motor-car and see the sights of Fairyland?' said the giant.

'Ooh, yes!' cried the children. So the giant took them out to his great motor-car, and they climbed into it. What a time they had! They saw elves and fairies, brownies and gnomes, pixies and witches, and all kinds of strange little folk. They went into glittering palaces, they had dinner with a wizard and tea with a brownie, so you can guess what a glorious day they had. They were sorry when half-past five came, and the giant took them back to his castle.

He took them up to the roof and showed them a chimney to hide behind. Then he shook hands with both of them, and thanked them very much for all their help.

'Thank you for the lovely day you've given us,' said the children. 'We only wish we could stay longer, but our mother would be worried if we did.'

'Sh! Here comes the goblin!' said Big-One, suddenly. He ran down the stairs, and the children were left alone behind their chimney. They heard a whirring sound, and saw the red and yellow aeroplane flying down, its strange wings flapping as it came.

The goblin landed neatly on the roof and ran to the stairs.

'Where's my sack of gold, Big-One?' he cried.

'Come down and fetch it!' came the giant's booming voice. 'It's in my cellar.'

The goblin raced down the stairs. As soon as he was gone Robert and Jill ran to the aeroplane and climbed into it. Robert pressed the button marked 'Up', and the aeroplane at once rose upwards. Then he pressed the button marked 'Home', and the machine turned round in the air and flew steadily towards the setting sun.

Jill looked back and saw the goblin standing on the roof of the castle, shouting wildly. The giant stood beside him, laughing. They could hear his great 'Ho-ho-ho' for a long way.

The aeroplane flew steadily onwards. Suddenly Jill gave a cry and pointed downwards.

'There's our house, Robert!' she cried. 'Press the 'Down' button quickly!'

Robert pressed it. The aeroplane swooped down and landed on the hillside where the children had sat learning their lessons that morning. Robert and Jill jumped out, picked up their books which were still where they had left them, and raced home.

'Why, my dears, wherever have you been?' cried their mother. 'I have been so worried about you!'

'Oh Mummy, we've had such an adventure!' cried Robert. 'We've been up in a goblin aeroplane!' and he told her all that happened.

Their mother was so astonished that she simply couldn't say a word.

'Come and see the aeroplane,' said Robert. 'It's out on the hillside.'

They all three ran to the hill – but just as they got there they heard a whirring sound and Robert pointed up in the air.

'There it goes!' he cried. 'I expect it's gone back to the goblin. Oh, Mummy, I wish you'd seen all the buttons inside, and had come for a ride with us.'

'But that's not an aeroplane,' said their mother. 'It's only a very big bird. I can see its wings flapping.'

'No, really, it's the goblin aeroplane,' said Jill. But I don't think their mother believed it.

'Anyhow, my dears,' she said, as they all went home again. 'What a very good thing it was that you were good and learnt your lessons properly this morning – else you might have had to stay with that giant!'

And it was a good thing, wasn't it?

The
Little Pink Pig

THERE was once a little pink pig who lived with his mother and nine other piglets in a comfortable sty. His name was Curly because he had such a twisty tail, and he was a very plump little fellow indeed.

But he was not as good as the others. He was always grumbling because he couldn't go into the fields with the cows, and couldn't go on the pond with the ducks.

'Be content,' said his mother. 'You are a little pig, not a cow or a duck. You should be happy to live at peace in a nice comfortable sty.'

'Pigs are silly creatures!' said the little pig rudely. 'They do nothing but grunt! I wish I wasn't a pig! I have a good mind to run away and be something else!'

'Don't be foolish!' said his mother, and she gave him a push with her snout. 'Lie down by me and go to sleep in the nice warm sun.'

But the little pig wouldn't. He grunted crossly

and ran to the other side of the sty. The gate was there and the little pig looked underneath the lowest bar. The world seemed very exciting outside. There was Gobble the turkey making a tremendous noise. There was Dobbin the horse stamping with his foot. There was Rover the dog barking madly.

'Why was I born a little pink pig?' sighed Curly. 'If only I could live with Rover or Gobble or with the white ducks on the pond!'

He pushed his little snout farther under the gate and began to push himself through. Suddenly he slipped right underneath, and there he was in the farmyard!

'Ho!' said the little pink pig to himself. 'This is fine! This is the world! Now I shall no longer be a little pink pig, but I shall be a turkey or a dog or a horse. I will go to Dobbin and ask him to teach me to be a horse.'

So he trotted over to Dobbin, who was most surprised to see Curly in the farmyard.

'Please, said Curly, 'I want to be a horse. Pigs are silly creatures. Tell me what I must do to be a horse.'

Dobbin thought that the little pink pig was very foolish.

'You must neigh like this!' he said, and he

put his head down and neighed loudly in Curly's ear. The little pig fell over with fright.

'Then you must kick like this!' said Dobbin, and he kicked out with his hind legs, sending the little pink pig right up into the air. Curly came down with a splash in the pond. How frightened he was!

'Quack!' said the ducks swimming round. 'Quack!'

'Oh, I won't be a horse!' said Curly. 'They are horrid creatures. I will be a duck!'

So he spoke to the surprised ducks round him.

'Please,' he said, 'I want to be a duck. Pigs are silly creatures. Tell me what I must do to be a duck.'

The ducks thought that the little pink pig was very foolish.

'You must quack like this,' they said, and they all crowded round him, quacking so loudly that he was nearly deafened.

'Then you must peck like this!' they said, and began pecking him all over his body till he grunted in terror and ran out of the water as fast as ever he could.

'Oh, I won't be a duck!' cried Curly in a rage. 'They are horrid creatures. I will be a dog.'

So he went to where old Rover the yard-dog lay half in and half out of his kennel.

'Please,' he said. 'I want to be a dog. Pigs are silly creatures. Tell me what I must do to be a dog.'

Rover thought that the little pink pig was very foolish.

'You must bark like this!' he said, and made such a loud noise in Curly's ear that the pig turned pale with fright.

'Then you must bite like this!' said the dog, and bit Curly's tail very hard indeed. The little

pig squeaked loudly and ran away in a great hurry.

'Oh, I won't be a dog!' he cried in a temper. 'Dogs are horrid creatures. I will be a farmer!'

He saw Mr Straws the Farmer in the distance, and ran up to him. He thought it would be very grand to be a man and own everything on the farm.

'Please,' he said, 'I want to be a farmer. Pigs are silly creatures. Tell me what I must do to be a farmer.'

Mr Straws thought that the little pink pig was very foolish.

'You must shout like this!' he said, and he shouted at Curly so loudly that the pig ran away.

'Then you must punish naughty pigs like this!' said the farmer, and he began to spank Curly with his big stick. The little pig ran faster and came at last to his sty. He squeezed under the lowest bar and fled to his mother.

His mother grunted softly. All the other piglets squeaked happily, and rooted about in the straw. The sun shone warmly. The sty looked very comfortable and happy.

The little pink pig looked about him, and grunted.

'Oh, I have been very foolish,' he sighed.

'How lovely it is to hear grunts instead of barks and quacks! How comfortable my sty is! What sweet creatures pigs are! How glad I am to be a piglet and not a horrid horse, or dog or duck!'

And the little pink pig settled down to be a good pig, and was happy ever afterwards.

The Runaway Toys

DIANE and David had more toys than any other children in the town. Their playroom was full of dolls, teddy-bears, a toy clown, soldiers, Noah's arks, balls, trains and bricks. You would think they were happy, contented children with such a lovely lot of playthings, but they weren't.

They were spoilt, disagreeable children, very unkind to their dolls and teddies, and not a bit generous with all their toys. Diane would rather break a doll than give it away, and David would stamp on his soldiers rather than give a boxful to some child who had no toys at all.

So you can guess what kind of children they were. Their toys hated them, and trembled whenever Diane and David came into the playroom.

'I'm afraid Diane will pull off my arm,' said a pretty doll.

'I'm afraid David will tear off my nose,' whispered the clown.

'Diane might break us all,' groaned the Noah's ark animals.

'And David will certainly overwind me and break my spring,' said the clockwork train, with a sigh.

Now one evening, half an hour before bedtime, Diane and David had a quarrel. Diane wanted to play with David's soldiers, and he wouldn't let her. So she snatched a boxful away from him, and shouted that she was going to have them.

'If you take my soldiers, I'll take your dolls!' said Tom in a rage, and he pounced on a baby doll and a pretty talking doll.

Then what a fight there was! Diane smacked David and David punched Diane and pulled her hair. The soldiers were trodden on and broken, the two dolls lay trembling on their faces, one with its arm broken and the other with its dress torn to rags. David kicked the clown into a corner and Diane trod heavily on a teddy-bear, who growled angrily.

Soon their mother came running into the room wondering what the noise was.

'You naughty children!' she cried. 'You shall

both go to bed at once! Just look at your poor toys!'

The children had to go to bed there and then, and the toys were left scattered all over the floor. There they lay until the clock struck twelve.

As soon as the last stroke died away, the clown sat up and looked round.

'Well, toys!' he said, in a mournful voice, 'what a dreadful evening this has been!'

The dolls sat up and so did the teddy-bear. The baby doll cried because her arm was broken, and the clown tied it up gently for her.

'I do think Diane and David are just the worst children in the world!' said the talking doll, angrily, looking at her torn frock. 'I wish we didn't belong to them!'

'So do I!' said Mr Noah, climbing out of the ark, and looking sadly at some of his broken animals on the floor.

'Well, why should we stop with them!' said the captain of the soldiers. 'Here's half my men wounded by those unkind children! I declare I won't stay with them a day longer!'

'Ooh!' said all the toys in wonder. 'But how can we go away? We've nowhere to go to!'

'We needn't bother about where to go,' said Mr Noah, excitedly. 'The first thing is to go!'

'I'll take you!' said the clockwork train importantly. 'I think there's enough room in my carriages for most of you, only you'll have to take the roofs off, because you're too big, most of you, to get in through the doors.'

What an excitement there was in the playroom. Six dolls, two teddy-bears, twenty-two soldiers, all Mr Noah's family and animals, and a woolly sheep managed to get into the train, after Mr Noah had slid the roofs off all the carriages. It was a dreadful squeeze, but nobody minded.

Then the clown wound up the train and jumped into the cab to drive it. Off they went over the playroom floor, and out through the door. Down the passage they ran, the wheels making no noise at all on the carpet. The side-door swung open to let them through, and the train ran into the garden, puffing and panting with its load of happy toys.

Down the road it ran, passing a most astonished policeman, who could hardly believe his eyes. Then it turned down a lane, and came to a stop. The clown got out and wound the train up again and once more it started off. It ran for a very long way, and at last said that it was really getting very tired, and what about finding somewhere to stop for the night?

'There's a cottage near by,' said the clown. 'Let's go and see if any children are there, and if they look nice or not.'

So off went the train again and stopped just outside the cottage. The clown and the teddy-bears climbed up on the window sill and looked in. It was a very poor cottage, and inside the room the toys could see three children lying asleep in a bed. The moon shone on a rag doll that the biggest child was cuddling.

On a table near by was a piece of paper with a beautiful train drawn on it.

'The boy must have done that,' whispered the clown. 'He must be fond of trains.'

The youngest child of all held a very old rabbit in her arms. It had lost one ear and its tail, but it looked very happy because the little girl loved it.

'That's all the toys they've got!' said the clown. 'They look kind children, and I expect they would love us. Shall we climb in at the window and put ourselves on the bed ready for them to see when they wake up?'

Everyone agreed, and one by one the toys climbed in through the window. It was a difficult job hauling the train up with all the carriages, but it was done at last, and soon the moon shone down on a bedful of toys waiting quietly for the daytime.

When the sun shone in through the window, the three children woke up. The boy sat up and yawned. Then he suddenly saw all the dolls, teddy-bears, the clown, soldiers and everything, and he blinked in amazement, thinking he was still asleep.

'Ooh, look!' he cried to his sisters. 'See what's on our bed!'

The little girls woke up and cried out in surprise. One of them picked up a doll and hugged her, and the other cuddled the clown. The boy picked up the clockwork train and looked at it admiringly.

'Mummy, Mummy!' called the children. 'Where did all these toys come from? Did you put them there?'

Their mother came into the room and stared in astonishment at all the toys.

'No,' she said. 'Why, my dears, I couldn't possibly afford to buy you even one of them, and no one would give me so many as that for you!'

'Well, where did they come from, then?' wondered the children. 'Aren't they beautiful? Can we keep them, Mummy? We'll take such care of them.'

'I know you will,' said their mother. 'But what puzzles me is where they came from.'

'Perhaps Santa Claus sent them, and forgot it wasn't Christmas,' said the little girl.

'That must be it!' said the boy. 'Well, we'll look after them well, and won't we be proud of them!'

They kept their word. The toys had never been so well-cared-for or so much loved. They were as happy as the day was long, and never, never wanted to leave the ugly little cottage and go back to the fine playroom they had left.

And what about Diane and David? They were surprised to find nearly all their toys gone when they went into the playroom next morning. They looked for this and they looked for that, but it wasn't any good – the toys were gone.

'Well, it serves you right,' said their mother, sternly. 'You didn't know how to treat your toys, and I expect Santa Claus came along and took them away from you!'

'He didn't!' said Diane, beginning to cry. 'Oh, I wish they hadn't gone. I won't be so horrid again, Mummy, I really won't! Then perhaps the toys will come back.'

But, as you will guess, they never did!

A Puppy in Wonderland

CHIPS was a round, fat little puppy. He belonged to Alan, James and Kate, and they were all very fond of him. He was rather naughty, because he would chew slippers up, and dig great holes in the garden.

'He's a dear little chap,' said Alan, 'but I do wish he'd stop digging in the garden. Daddy is getting so cross!'

'Let's take him for a walk,' said Kate. 'If we make him tired out, he will go to sleep in his basket, and won't get into any more mischief.'

So they called Chips, and he came bounding up to them, delighted to think that he was going for a walk.

'Where shall we go?' asked Alan.

'Through Heyho Wood,' said James. 'It's such a hot day, and it will be nice and cool there.'

So off they started. It was hot! The sun shone

down, and there was not a cloud in the sky. They were glad to get into the shady wood.

Chips ran here and there, sniffing at the ground in great excitement. He could smell rabbits! Then he saw one! Oh, my goodness, what a to-do there was! He yelped and barked, and tore off as fast as his short legs would let him, tripping and tumbling over blackberry brambles as he went!

'Chips! Chips! Come here, you'll get lost!' cried Alan. But Chips took no notice at all. On he went, bounding through the trees, his little tail wagging like mad. He must catch that rabbit, he really must!

But of course he didn't! The rabbit went diving headlong into its hole, and when Chips came up and looked round there was no bunny to be seen!

'It must have gone into the ground like worms do!' thought the puppy. So he chose a nice green place, and began to dig. He scrabbled the earth with his front paws, and sent it flying out behind him with his back ones. He puffed and panted, snorted and sneezed, and he took no notice at all of the shouts and whistles of the children some distance away.

Suddenly there came a shout of rage. Chips

looked up in surprise, and what did he see but a brownie, dressed in a brown tunic, long stockings and a pointed hat! He was staring at Chips with a very angry look on his face, and the puppy wondered why. He didn't wonder long, because he suddenly remembered the rabbit again, and once more began to dig madly.

That made the brownie crosser than ever. He took a long green whistle from his pocket and blew seven short blasts on it. Immediately a crowd of little men like himself came up.

'Look!' said the first brownie, fiercely. 'Look at that horrid dog! He's dug a hole right in the very middle of the fairy ring which we got ready for the Queen's dance tonight! And he won't stop, either!'

'Stop! Stop, you naughty dog!' cried all the brownies. 'Stop digging at once!'

But Chips took no notice at all. He just went on digging. The brownies didn't know what to do.

'He may bite if we go too near him,' said one. 'But we must catch him and punish him. Why, the Queen won't be able to have her midnight dance tonight!'

'I know how we can get him!' cried a small brownie. 'Let's go and ask the spiders to give

us some of their web! Then we'll throw it round the dog and catch him like that!'

'That's a good idea!' cried all the little men. 'Then we'll take him to prison.'

Chips looked up. He thought the brownies looked very cross indeed. He decided that he would go and find the children. But the brownies had closed round him in a ring, and he could see no way to get through. Then two or three of them came running up with a large net made of sticky spider thread. They suddenly threw it over the puppy – and poor Chips was caught!

He tried to get out of the web, but he couldn't. The brownies dragged him away, and he yelped miserably. The children heard him yelping, and looked at one another.

'Chips is in trouble!' said Kate. 'Quick, come and see what's the matter!'

The three children ran as fast as they could to where they heard the puppy yelping. But when they got there, there was no Chips to be seen. There was only a cross-looking brownie filling in a newly-dug hole.

'Oh!' said the children in surprise, and stopped to look at the funny little man. He looked at them, too, and then went on with his work.

'I suppose you haven't seen our puppy, have you?' asked Kate, at last.

'Oh, so it was your dog, was it?' said the brownie. 'Well, do you know what he has done? Do you see this ring of fine green grass, surrounded by toadstools? It was got ready for a dance tonight, by order of the Queen – and your horrid little dog dug a great big hole in the middle of it. It's all spoilt!'

'Oh dear, I am sorry,' said Alan. 'He really is naughty to do that – but I'm sure he didn't mean any harm. He's only a puppy, you know. He's not four months old yet.'

'Well, he's been taken to prison,' said the brownie. 'He wouldn't even stop when we told him to!'

Kate began to cry. She couldn't bear to think of poor little Chips being taken to prison. Alan put his arm round her.

'Don't worry, Kate,' he said. 'We'll find some way of rescuing him.'

The brownie laughed.

'Oh, no, you won't!' he said. 'We shan't set him free until he's sorry.'

He ran off, and disappeared between the trees. The children stared at one another in dismay.

'We must find Chips!' said Kate. 'Where can they have put him?'

'Look, here are the marks of their footsteps,' said James pointing to where the grass was trodden down. 'Let's follow their tracks as far as we can.'

So they set off. Chips had been carried by the brownies, so they could find no marks of his toes, but they could easily follow the traces left on the long grass by the crowd of brownies.

Through the trees they went, keeping their eyes on the ground. Suddenly the tracks stopped.

'That's funny!' said Alan. 'Where can they all have gone to? Look! They stop quite suddenly just here, in the middle of this little clearing.'

'Perhaps they've flown into the air,' suggested Kate.

'I don't think so,' said Alan. 'That little fellow we met had no wings.'

'Well, did they go down through the ground, then?' wondered James. He looked hard at the grass, and then gave a cry of excitement.

'Look!' he said. 'I do believe there's a trap-door here, with grass growing neatly all over it!'

The children looked down – yes, James was

right. There was a square patch there, which might well be a trap-door.

Alan knelt down, and after a few minutes he found out how to lift up the trap-door. James and Kate looked down the opening in excitement. They saw a tiny flight of steps leading into darkness. Alan took out his torch and flashed it into the hole.

'Look!' he cried, and picked up a white hair. 'Here's one of Chip's hairs. Now we know they took him down this way! Come on!'

The three children scrambled down. There were twenty steps, and then a stone platform. To their great astonishment they saw an underground river flowing by.

'Well, Chips must have gone this way because there's no other way for him to go!' said James. 'But how are we to follow! There's no boat to take us.'

But just at that moment a little blue boat floated up, and came to the platform, where it stayed quite still.

'Hurrah!' said Alan. 'Here's just what we want. Come on, you others.'

They all jumped in at once, and the little boat floated away down the dark stream. After a while it came out into the open air, and the children were very glad.

They looked round them in wonder.

'This must be Wonderland!' said Kate. 'Look at all the beautiful castles and palaces!'

'And look at the funny higgledy-piggledy cottages everywhere!' said James.

'And what a crowd of different kinds of fairyfolk!' said Alan. 'Look, brownies, elves, pixies, gnomes, and lots of others!'

'I wonder where the brownies took Chips,' said Kate. 'Shall we ask someone and see if they know?'

'Yes,' said Alan. So they stopped the boat by guiding it gently to the bank, and then asked a passing pixie if he had seen any brownies with a puppy dog.

'Yes,' he said. 'They had him wrapped up in spider's web, and took him to that castle over there.'

He pointed to a castle near by on a steep hill.

'Thank you,' said Alan. Then he turned to the others. 'Come on,' he said. 'We must leave this boat, and make for the castle.'

Out they all jumped, and took the path that led to the castle. It was not long before they were climbing the hill on which the castle stood.

They came to a great gate, and by it hung a bellrope.

Alan pulled it, and at once a jangling noise was heard in the courtyard beyond. The gate swung open, and the children went in, feeling a little bit frightened.

There was no one in the courtyard. Exactly opposite was a door, which stood open. The children went towards it and peeped inside. Just as they got there they heard a sorrowful bark.

'Chips is here!' said Kate, in a whisper. 'Let's go in.'

They crept inside the door, and found themselves in a big hall. At one end was a raised platform on which stood a very grand chair, almost a throne. On it was sitting a very solemn brownie. In front of him, still tied up in the spider's thread, was poor Chips, very much afraid. Round him were scores of little brownies, and they were telling the chief one what he had done.

Kate ran right up to the solemn brownie, and James and Alan followed.

'Please, please let our puppy go!' begged Kate. 'He didn't mean any harm to your fairy ring. He was after a rabbit, that's all.'

'What sort of rabbit?' asked the chief brownie.

'Oh, a big sandy one, with white tips to its ears,' said Alan. 'I saw it just as it ran away from Chips.'

'Then he's a good puppy, not a naughty one!' cried the solemn brownie. 'That rabbit is very bad. It used to draw the Queen's carriage, and what do you think it did?'

'What?' asked the three children.

'Why, one night, it ran away with the carriage and all!' said the brownie. 'The poor Queen was so frightened. The carriage turned over, and she was thrown out. The rabbit ran off, and we have never been able to catch it since.'

'Well, Chips nearly caught it!' said Kate, eagerly. 'And I expect he saw it go into a burrow, and tried to dig it out – only he chose the wrong place, that's all. I'm sure he's very sorry indeed for all the trouble he has caused.'

'Wuff-wuff! Wuff-wuff!' said Chips, sitting on his back legs, and begging for mercy.

'We'll let him go at once!' cried the brownies, and two of them ran to cut away the web that bound him. In a trice Chips was free, and danced delightedly round the three children. Kate picked him up and hugged him.

'Take them back to the wood,' commanded the chief brownie. 'And give Chips a bone to make up for his fright.'

The puppy barked in glee when a large bone was given to him. He picked it up in his mouth and began to chew it.

'The carriage is at the door,' said a little brownie, running in. The children were taken to the great door, and outside in the yard stood a grand carriage of silver and gold, driven by a brownie driver. Six small white horses drew the carriage. How excited the children were!

They all got in, said goodbye to the brownies, and then off went the carriage at a smart pace. It went up hill and down dale, through miles of Wonderland, and at last entered the same wood in which their adventures had started that morning.

'Thank you so much,' said the children, as they jumped out. They patted the horses, and then the carriage turned round and was soon out of sight.

The children walked home, and told their mother all that had happened. But she found it very difficult to believe them.

'Are you sure you haven't made it all up?' she asked.

'Well, look, here is the bone that the brownies gave to Chips!' said Kate. 'And look at his tail! It's still covered with spider's web!'

So it was – and after that their mother had to believe their exciting story, especially as Chips had learnt his lesson, and never, never, never, dug a hole in the garden again!

Snifty's
Lamp Post

ONCE upon a time there lived a very disagreeable gnome called Snifty. He was head of the gnome village he lived in, and he was very unkind to everyone.

Now, the Chancellor of Gnomeland came to visit him one night. There was no moon, and it was so dark that the Chancellor could hardly see his way through the village. He drove down the wrong path, and when he got out of his carriage to see where he was, he fell over two or three geese, and then sat down on a frightened pig.

This made him very cross, and when he got to Snifty's house he told him that he ought to be ashamed of having a village which was so dreadfully dark.

'Why don't you have a fine new lamp post put just in front of your house?' he asked. 'Then your visitors would know where you lived, and would not fall over pigs and geese.'

'I will,' said Snifty, rubbing his hands gleefully, glad to think that his villagers would have to buy a fine lamp post for him out of their own money. He didn't once think of buying it himself. He always made his poor people pay for everything, and because they were afraid of him, they did not dare to say no.

So the next day he sent a notice round the village to say that the gnomes were to make him a fine new lamp post. Then when the Chancellor paid him a call another night he wouldn't go the wrong way.

'Will you give us the money for it?' asked the gnomes.

'Certainly not!' answered Snifty. 'What is the use of being the chief if I can't get things for nothing, I should like to know?'

The gnomes knew that it was of no use to say anything more, but they were very angry.

'It's time we made Snifty stop this sort of thing,' they grumbled. 'He's always expecting us to pay for everything, and he never gives us a penny towards it.'

They began to make the lamp post. It was a lovely one, for the gnomes liked making things as beautiful as they could, no matter whether they were working for people they liked or disliked.

Snifty soon sent them word that the

Chancellor was coming to see him again, and he ordered the gnomes to have the lamp post put up in time.

Then the gnomes grumbled even more, and suddenly they decided that they would do just what Snifty said, and no more. They would finish the lamp post and put it up – but they wouldn't put any oil in the lamp, or light it! That would just serve old Snifty right!

So they finished the lamp post and put it up just in front of Snifty's front gate. He watched them from the window, but he didn't bother to come out and say thank you.

The Chancellor arrived that evening, and again it was very, very dark. No one had put any oil in the lamp or lighted it, so there was no light for him to see by again. He was very cross, especially when his carriage got stuck in the ditch and couldn't be moved. He got out, and trod on a hedgehog, which hurt him very much.

'Why doesn't Snifty do as I tell him, and get a lamp post put in front of his gate?' he growled. 'He's rich enough!'

Snifty was very angry when he found that the lamp was not lighted. The Chancellor told him how his carriage had stuck in the ditch, and asked him why it was that he had not got his lamp lighted, to show him the way. Snifty rang a bell, and told his servant to fetch some of the village gnomes, and he would hear why they had disobeyed him.

The gnomes soon came, and Snifty asked them angrily why they had not obeyed him.

'We have obeyed you, Sir,' answered the gnomes. 'You told us to put a lamp post in front of your gate, and we have done so. But you did not tell us to put any oil in it.'

'Oh, you silly, stupid creatures!' cried Snifty, angrily. 'Then hear me now. The Chancellor is coming again tomorrow night, and oil is to be put in the lamp. Do you hear?'

'Yes,' said the gnomes, and went out.

When they had got to their homes they put their heads together and decided that they would again do exactly as Snifty had said – they would put oil in the lamp, but no wick!

So next day oil was poured into the lamp, but no wick was put in. And when the Chancellor arrived that night he again found that he could not see where Snifty lived! This time he jumped out of his carriage too soon, and walked straight into a very muddy pond. He was so angry when he reached Snifty's at last that he could hardly speak.

Once again Snifty called the gnomes to his house, and asked them what they meant by not obeying him.

'Sir, we have obeyed you,' answered the gnomes. 'We have put oil in the lamp as you bade us. You did not tell us to put in a wick – so how could the lamp be lighted?'

'Then put in a wick' shouted Snifty, very angry indeed.

So next day the gnomes put a fine big wick into the lamp, but when evening came, they did not light it.

'Snifty said "put in a wick" – he did not say

60

light the wick,' said the gnomes grinning among themselves.

This time the Chancellor was so certain that the lamp would be alight that he drove right through the village without seeing it, looking all the time for Snifty's lighted lamp. When he stopped and asked where he was, he found that he had driven three miles beyond the village. So he had to turn his carriage round and go back.

'Are you disobeying me on purpose?' he asked Snifty, when he at last arrived. 'Where is that lamp?'

'Isn't it lighted?' cried Snifty.

'No, it isn't,' answered the Chancellor.

'Then I'll find out why!' cried Snifty in a rage, and he called in the gnomes once more.

'Why have you disobeyed me again?' he shouted angrily.

'We have not disobeyed you!' answered the gnomes in surprise. 'You told us to put a wick in the lamp, and we have done so. We did not hear you order us to light the wick.

'Then tomorrow light the wick!' roared Snifty.

The gnomes consulted among themselves, and decided that the next night they would light the wick as Snifty had commanded, and then blow it out! So they would be obeying him, and yet he still would not have his light.

They did this. One of them lighted the lamp carefully, and then after five minutes he blew the light out. Then they waited for the Chancellor to come as usual.

This time the Chancellor was so angry to find that the lamp was again not lighted for him that he almost deafened Snifty with his shouting. Snifty called in the gnomes again, and they explained that he had told them to light the lamp, and they had done so. He had not told them to let it burn all night long, and as oil was expensive they had blown out the light after five minutes.

Snifty was too furious to speak for a whole minute.

'Tomorrow you will light the wick which rests in the oil, and you will see that the lamp is burning all night long,' he cried at last. 'I will have no misunderstanding this time.'

The gnomes went away. For some time they could not think of any way in which they might again trick Snifty, and yet still obey him. Then one of them had a good idea.

'Snifty didn't say anything about where the

lamp was to be, did he?' he said. 'Let's move it away from his gate when night comes, and put it somewhere else. We'll light it, and keep it burning all night long – but it won't be in the right place!'

The other gnomes thought this was a splendid idea. So when night came, they went quietly to where the lamp post was, and carried it away to the other end of the village, and there they lighted it.

Very soon the Chancellor came by, and seeing the light, he stopped and got out of his carriage. He was very much puzzled when he could see no sign of Snifty's house. He stopped a little gnome and asked him.

'Oh, Snifty lives at the other end of the village,' answered the gnome.

'Oh dear, oh dear!' said the Chancellor. 'What a nuisance! I have got the King of Gnomeland in my carriage tonight, and I didn't want to lose my way as I usually do. I told Snifty to be sure and have the lamp alight outside his front gate, so that I would know where I was.'

Now when the little gnome heard that the King was in the carriage, he was very much surprised. In a trice he had told the other gnomes, and very quickly they lifted up the lamp post and carried it in front of the carriage to show the driver the way. They set the lamp down by Snifty's front gates, and then cheered the King loudly as he drove by.

'What very nice, good-natured fellows,' said the King, pleased. 'Snifty is lucky to have such fine people in his village.'

When they reached the house, the Chancellor told Snifty that again there had been no lamp outside his house, and sternly asked him why. Snifty gasped with rage, and called in his gnomes at once.

'Why have you disobeyed me again?' he cried.

'We haven't disobeyed,' answered the gnomes. 'You told us to light the lamp, and keep it burning all night long. But you didn't say it was to be outside your gates.'

Then Snifty lost his temper, and said some rude and horrid things to the gnomes in front of the King. The King stopped him and asked to be told all the tale. When he found that night after night Snifty had been tricked over the lamp, he was very much puzzled.

'But your villagers seem such good-natured fellows,' he said. 'Why, they carried the lamp all the way in front of my carriage for me! It is very wrong of them to behave like this. After all, it is your lamp, for you have paid for it, Snifty. They have no right to treat it like that.'

'Excuse me, Your Majesty,' said a gnome, stepping forward. 'We had to pay for the lamp, not Snifty. He makes us pay for everything he wants. If he had paid for the lamp himself, we should not have tried to teach him a lesson.'

'Are you poor?' the King asked Snifty.

'No, Your Majesty,' said Snifty, beginning to tremble.

'Then why do you not pay for your lamp yourself?' asked the King. 'Many tales have reached me lately, Snifty, of your meanness, and I came here to find out if they were true or not. I now see very plainly that they are. Your people were quite right to treat you as you deserve. You must leave the village, and I will make someone else the chief!'

So Snifty had to go, and you may be sure nobody missed him. As for the lamp, it now burns brightly outside the new chief's gates every night, and reminds him to be kind and generous. If he isn't, I don't know what trick the gnomes would play on him – but I'm quite sure they would think of something!

The Clockwork Duck

THERE was once a clockwork duck who thought a very great deal of herself. She was made of plastic and floated beautifully. She had a little key in her side, and when she was wound up she paddled herself along in the water.

She lived in the soap dish by the bath, along

with the soap, a sponge, a floating goldfish and a little green frog. When Harry had his bath at night the clockwork duck always swam up and down and made him laugh. Mummy used to wind her up, and when she was paddling herself along, the frog and the goldfish, who could only float, thought she was very wonderful indeed.

'You ought to go out on the pond with the real ducks,' said the frog. 'My, wouldn't they think you marvellous.'

'Yes, you are wasted here,' said the goldfish. 'You should go out into the world.'

The clockwork duck listened, and began to long to go out to the real ducks on the pond.

'They would be so proud to have me with them,' she thought. 'Perhaps they would make me their queen! I am very pretty, and when I am wound up I can swim very fast indeed!'

The more she thought about it, the more she wanted to go. And one day, when Spot the dog came into the bathroom, she called to him and begged him to take her down to the pond in his mouth.

'Very well,' said Spot, in surprise. 'But you'll be sorry you left your nice home in the soap dish, I can tell you! Real ducks haven't any time for clockwork ones!'

He picked up the little duck in his mouth, ran downstairs, went out of the back door, and took the duck to the edge of the pond. He dropped her into the water and left her there.

Soon a large white duck swam up and looked at the clockwork duck.

'What are you?' she said.

'A clockwork duck,' said the duck. 'I am a very wonderful duck. I have a key in my side, and when it is wound up I can swim across the water.'

'Well, I can swim over the pond without being wound up at all!' said the duck. 'I don't think that is very wonderful!'

'You don't know what you are talking about!' said the clockwork duck, crossly. 'You ought to make me queen of the pond, that's what you ought to do! I tell you I am a very marvellous bird!'

By this time other ducks had swum up and were listening to the clockwork duck. Then a frog popped up his green head, and two or three fishes looked out of the water too. The clockwork duck felt that she was making quite a success.

'Wind me up and see how nicely I can swim,' she said.

So the frog swam up to her, took the key in his front fingers and wound her up. Whir-r-r-r, she went, and her legs began to paddle to and fro, sending her quickly over the water.

All the ducks, frogs and fishes laughed to see her, and she was proud to think she had amused them.

'Well, she said at last, 'would you like to make me your queen?'

'You must prove that you are worthy to be a queen first,' said the big white duck. 'Listen – we big ducks want to swim down the pond and get into the little brook, because we have heard that there is plenty of food to be found in the mud there. But we don't want the little yellow ducklings to go with us.'

'Well, I'll look after them for you, and keep them safe,' said the clockwork duck, proudly. 'Just wind me up once more and I shall be all right.'

So they wound her up, and then swam off to the little brook that ran by the end of the pond. The yellow ducklings swam up to look at the clockwork duck who was to look after them, and when they saw that she was no bigger than they were, they laughed.

'Why, you can't be any older than we are,'

they cried. 'We don't want to be looked after by you!'

'You stay with me and be good,' said the clockwork duck, fiercely.

'No,' said the ducklings. 'We want to go after the big ducks and see what food they are finding in the brook. Good-bye!'

With that the naughty little ducklings swam off. The clockwork duck swam after them as fast as she could, but alas! – long before she reached the brook her clockwork ran down, and she could paddle no farther. She could not quack like a real duck, so all she could do was to bob up and down on the ripples, hoping that no harm would come to the yellow ducklings.

Soon she heard a great noise of quacking, and back to the pond came the big ducks with the little ducklings behind them, looking very sorry for themselves.

'What do you mean by letting our ducklings swim off by themselves like that?' quacked the biggest duck, in a temper. 'Do you know that a rat has caught one, and that another got caught in the weeds and couldn't get free!'

'Why didn't you peck them and make them behave?' cried another duck.

'I can't peck,' said the clockwork duck.

'Well, why didn't you swim with them and see that no harm came to them?' shouted a third duck.

'I tried to, but my clockwork ran down, and I couldn't swim any farther,' said the clockwork duck, hanging her head.

'Well, you could have at least have quacked loudly, so that we should have known something was happening, and could have come to your help!' said the first duck, fiercely.

'But I can't quack!' said the poor clockwork duck.

'Then what use are you!' cried all the ducks, in a rage. 'You're the stupidest, silliest creature we've ever seen, and as for making you our queen, why, we'd sooner ask that dog over there!'

They swam at the frightened duck, and pecked her so hard that little dents came here and there in her plastic skin. Their quacking disturbed Spot the dog, who was lying asleep in the sunshine. He jumped up and ran to the clockwork duck's rescue.

In a trice he picked her up in his mouth and ran off with her.

'Take me back to my nice home in the soap

dish,' sobbed the poor little duck. 'I don't like the big outside world.'

So Spot ran upstairs and put her gently back into the soap dish with her good friends the goldfish, the sponge and the soap. They were sorry to hear her sad story.

'Never mind, you shall be our queen!' they said. 'But hush! Here comes Harry for his bath!'

Harry trotted into the bathroom, and Mummy ran the water into the bath. She picked up the clockwork duck and wound her up.

'Oh, Mummy!' cried Harry, in surprise. 'Look, how dented and spotted my little duck is! What has done that?'

But Mummy didn't know – and you may be sure that the clockwork duck said never a word!

A Cat
in Fairyland

BIMBO was a big black cat, the finest puss in town. His whiskers were four inches long, his tail was fat and furry. His coat shone like silk, and his purr was so loud that it sounded like a motorbike out in the road!

He belonged to Jenny and Simon, and they loved him very much.

'He is the most beautiful puss I've ever seen,' said Jenny.

'If only he could talk, it would be lovely,' said Simon. 'He's so clever he could teach us a lot.'

Bimbo often used to go out for walks with Jenny and Simon. When they took their tea to Hallo Wood, Bimbo ran behind them, sat down with them, and shared their milk. Then he would go prowling off by himself, not very far away, always keeping the children well in sight.

One day all three started off, their tea in a basket. They went right to the middle of Hallo Wood, sat down and began their tea. When they

had finished Bimbo stalked off on his own, as usual. And suddenly a very strange thing happened.

Jenny happened to look up from the book she was reading and saw a strange little man, rather like a gnome, walking quietly through the trees. On his back he carried a large empty sack. Jenny nudged Simon and both children stared at the gnome in surprise and excitement, for they had never seen any kind of fairy before.

Bimbo didn't see the gnome. He was sitting down, washing himself, purring very loudly. The gnome crept up behind him, opened his large sack, and suddenly flung it right over Bimbo.

Jenny and Simon jumped up at once, shouting angrily. The gnome turned and saw them. At once he pulled the mouth of the bag tight, threw it over his shoulder with poor Bimbo struggling inside, and ran off through the wood. Jenny and Simon followed, fearful and raging, wondering what the gnome wanted with their beautiful cat.

Panting and puffing the gnome tore through the wood, with Jenny and Simon after him. He ran into a thick bush, and when the children came up, he had disappeared. They couldn't see him anywhere.

'Oh, poor Bimbo!' said Jenny, almost crying. 'Where has he been taken to? Oh, Simon, we really must find him and rescue him.'

'Well, I don't see where the gnome has gone to,' said Simon, puzzled. He looked round and ran here and there, but there was no sign of the gnome.

'We'd better go home and tell Mummy,' he said. 'Come on.'

But they had lost their way! They couldn't find the path they had taken in following the gnome, and they were quite lost. Jenny began to feel frightened, and wondered if the gnome would come back and take them prisoner too, but Simon cheered her up, and said that he would fight a dozen gnomes if he could see them.

'There's a little path running along here,' he said to Jenny. 'We'd better follow it. It must lead somewhere.'

So they ran down it, and after some time they came to the prettiest little cottage they had ever seen, so small that it really didn't look much more than a large doll's house. Simon knocked at the yellow front door, and a pixie with silvery wings opened it. She looked so surprised to see them.

'We've lost our way,' said Simon, politely. 'Could you please help us?'

'Come in,' said the pixie. 'Mind your heads.'

They had to stoop down to go inside, for the door was so small. Inside the cottage were small chairs and a tiny table. It was the funniest little place. Jenny was half afraid of sitting down in case she broke the chair she sat on.

'Let me offer you a cup of tea,' said the pixie, and she hurried to her small fireplace and took a boiling kettle off the hob.

'Well, we've really had tea,' said Simon, 'but it would be nice to have a cup of pixie tea, so thank you very much, we will.'

Then while the pixie made sweet-smelling tea in a little flowery teapot, and set out tiny currant cakes, Simon and Jenny told her all about the gnome who had stolen Bimbo, their cat.

'Now did you ever hear such a thing!' said the pixie, in surprise. 'I'm sure I know where your puss has been taken.'

'Oh where?' asked the children at once.

'To the old wizard, Too-Tall,' said the pixie, handing the plate of buns to Jenny. 'I know that his last cat, who used to help him in his spells, ran away a little while ago, and he has been wanting another. That gnome you saw is his servant, and I expect he has been looking out for a good black cat. When he saw your Bimbo he captured him at once, and I expect he took him straight to his master, Too-Tall.'

'But Bimbo would hate to help anyone with spells,' said Jenny. 'He's just an ordinary cat, and he would be very unhappy to live away from us. The wizard has no right to take him!'

'Could we rescue him, do you think?' asked Simon. 'Where does this wizard live?'

'He lives in Runaway House, not very far from here,' said the pixie.

'What a funny name!' said the children.

'Well, it's a funny house,' said the pixie. 'It's got four little legs underneath it, and when the wizard wants to move, he just tells it to run where he wants it to, and the legs run away at once, taking the house with them.'

'Goodness me!' said Jenny, her eyes shining with excitement. 'Wouldn't I like to see it!'

'I'll take you there, if you like,' said the pixie, and she wrapped a little coat round her. 'But mind – don't make a noise when we get there, or the old wizard might put a spell on us.'

'Will we be able to rescue Bimbo, do you think?' asked Simon.

'We'll see when we get there,' said the pixie, opening the front door. 'Come along.'

She took them back to the thick bush where the gnome had disappeared. To the children's surprise they saw a little trap-door hidden under the bush. The pixie pulled it open, and all three of them climbed down some steps into an underground passage. Then for some way they walked in darkness, guided only by the pixie's voice in front of them. Soon a little lamp shone out, and Jenny and Simon saw a crowd of little doors in front of them.

The pixie opened a blue one and led the way into a small room, where a grey rabbit was writing at a desk. He looked up, and asked where they wanted to go.

'To Runaway House,' answered the pixie. The rabbit gave them each a green ticket, and told them to sit on three little toadstools in the corner. They all sat down and the rabbit pressed a button. In a trice the three toadstools shot upwards and Jenny and Simon clutched at the edges in surprise.

For a long time they went up and up, and at last the toadstools slowed down. They came to a stop inside another small room, where a second rabbit sat. He took their tickets, opened a door and showed them out into the sunshine.

'What an adventure!' said Simon, who was thoroughly enjoying himself. 'I did like riding on those toadstools!'

They were on a hillside, and the pixie pointed to a little house at the top, surrounded on three sides by trees, to shelter it from the wind.

'That's Runaway House,' she said. 'You can see the feet peeping from underneath it. When it runs it raises itself on its legs and goes off like lightning!'

The three made their way up to it, and the pixie tiptoed to a little window at the back. She peeped inside, and beckoned to the children. They crept up and looked in.

Bimbo was inside! He sat on the floor in the middle of a chalk ring, looking very angry and very miserable. His great tail swept the floor from side to side and his fine whiskers twitched angrily.

The wizard Too-Tall, a thin bent old man in a pointed hat, was standing opposite the cat, waving a long stick. He looked very cross. In a corner by the fireplace was the gnome who had stolen Bimbo, stirring something in a big pot.

'You must help me with my magic spells, or I

will turn you into a mouse!' said the wizard to Bimbo. And then to the children's enormous surprise, Bimbo opened his mouth and spoke.

'Are your spells all good ones?' he asked. 'For I tell you this, Master Wizard, no cat belonging to my honourable family would ever help in making a bad spell for witches or goblins to use!'

'I am not a good wizard,' said Too-Tall, with a horrid smile. 'I make my money by selling magic to witches, and if you are too grand to help me, my honourable cat, I shall have to do as I said, and turn you into a mouse. Then you will be hunted by your honourable family, and be punished for your stupidity.'

Poor Bimbo began to tremble, but he still would not agree to help Too-Tall, and the wizard grew impatient.

'I will give you one more chance,' he said at last. 'Unless you stand up on your hind legs, turn round twice and mew seven times loudly whilst I chant my magic words and wave my enchanted stick, you shall be changed into a little brown mouse!'

He began to wave his long stick and chant curious words, which made the little pixie outside shiver and shake. But Bimbo did not stand up and mew as he had been told. He sat there in the middle of the ring, looking very much frightened, but quite determined not to help the wicked old wizard.

Then Too-Tall lost his patience. He struck Bimbo with his stick, called out a magic word, and then laughed loudly – for the black cat suddenly vanished, and in its place cowered a tiny brown mouse.

'Now you see what your punishment is!' cried the wizard. 'Go, hide yourself away, miserable creature, and be sure that when I get another cat, you will be hunted for your life!'

The little mouse rushed away into a corner, and hid itself in an old slipper. Jenny and Simon could hardly believe their eyes when they saw that their lovely Bimbo had vanished, and in his place was a poor little mouse. Jenny began to cry, but Simon doubled up his fists, half inclined to go in and fight the wizard and gnome.

'Don't do anything foolish,' whispered the pixie, dragging the two away from the window. 'Hush, Jenny, don't cry, or the wizard will hear you, and he might quite easily change all of us into mice too.'

'But I must do something about poor Bimbo,' said Simon, fiercely.

'Well, I've got a plan,' said the pixie. 'Listen. We'll wait till darkness comes, and then borrow three spades from Tippy, an elf who lives near by. We'll dig a big hole just a little way down the hill. Then we'll all borrow trays and trumpets, and make a fearful noise outside the cottage. The wizard will wake in a fright and think a great army is marching against him. He will order his house to run away, and as the only way it can run is down the hill because there are trees on every other side, it will fall straight into the pit we have dug for it!'

'What then?' asked the children in excitement, thinking it was a marvellous plan.

'Well, I'll pop inside the house before the wizard has got over his fright, and get his enchanted stick,' said the pixie, delightedly. 'He's no good without that, you know. You, Simon, must get hold of the gnome and hold him tightly. You, Jenny, must pick up the little mouse. The wizard will probably run away, for he is an awful coward without his magic stick.'

'Go on, go on!' cried the children, their eyes shining.

'That's all,' said the pixie. 'We'll just run off to Tippy's, then, and I'll see what I can do about Bimbo for you.

Night was coming on, for the sun had gone down over the hill. The pixie led the way to a large toadstool on the other side of the hill. It had a little door in it and the pixie knocked. An elf opened the door, and peeped out.

'Who is it?' he asked.

'It's only Tuffy the Pixie,' said the pixie. 'Can you lend us three spades, Tippy?'

'Certainly,' said Tippy, and he took three little spades from a corner of his strange toadstool house. The pixie took them, said thank you, and ran off again with the children. They passed the wizard's house, which was now lighted inside by a swinging lamp, and went a little way down the hillside.

Then they began to dig. How they dug! The pixie said a little spell over their spades to make them work quickly, and the hole soon began to grow. The spades flew in and out, and the children got quite out of breath.

At last it was finished. The moon shone out in the sky, and the pixie said they had better wait for a big cloud to come before they carried out the next part of their plan, for if the house could see before it as it ran, it would run round the hole they had made, instead of into it.

'I'll take the spades back to Tippy's and

borrow a few trays and things,' whispered the pixie. 'You stay here, and watch to see that everything is all right.

It wasn't long before the pixie was back again. She had with her three trays, two trumpets and a large whistle. She giggled as she handed out the things to the children.

'What a shock the wizard will get!' she said. 'Now creep with me just outside the cottage, and when I say 'GO!' bang on your trays and blow your trumpets hard. I'll blow my whistle, and if we don't give the wizard the fright of his life, I shall be surprised!'

They all crept up to the cottage. 'GO!' suddenly shouted the pixie as soon as a cloud came over the moon. In a trice there was a most fearful noise! The trays clanged, the trumpets blared, the whistle blew, and in between all three shouted at the top of their voices.

The wizard was sitting at his table eating his supper with the gnome. When they heard the fearful din outside, the wizard leapt to his feet and turned very pale.

'It's the elfin army after us!' he shouted. 'House, house, find your feet, run away, fast and fleet!'

At once the house stood up on its four legs

and began to move. It raced down the hill, straight towards the big hole that the children and the pixie had dug.

Plonk! It fell right into it. Chimneys flew about, windows smashed, and the wizard and the gnome cried out in terror. They couldn't get out of the door because it was buried in the pit, so they tried to get out of the window.

'Come on!' cried the pixie. 'Into the house, all of you!'

Jenny and Simon rushed to the fallen house. They climbed in at one window, and the pixie climbed in at another. Jenny ran to the corner where she saw the frightened little mouse peeping out of a slipper. She picked it up and slipped it into her pocket.

Simon rushed at the gnome and held him tightly, then called to Jenny to tie him up with a piece of rope he saw lying by the fire. The pixie snatched up the wizard's enchanted stick with a cry of delight.

The old wizard had scrambled out of his window and was rushing down the hill in the moonlight. He was frightened out of his wits!

'Leave the gnome and come away now,' said the pixie. 'If that old wizard meets any witch he knows he may bring her back here, and that would be awkward.'

The three climbed out of the tumbled-down house and ran down the hillside to give back the trays, trumpets and whistle. As they came back again, the pixie pointed to the east with a shout of dismay.

'There's the wizard with two witches! Come on, we shall have to hurry.'

She took the children to the door that led to the toadstool room where the rabbit sat. In a twinkling they had their tickets and were sitting on three toadstools. Just as the strange lifts had started to rush downwards the wizard and witches came racing into the room, and sat down on other toadstools.

'Ooh, my, now we're in for a race!' groaned the pixie. 'Jump off your toadstools as soon as they stop and run for the door. Race down the passage and up the steps to the trap-door as fast as ever you can!'

So as soon as the toadstools stopped, Jenny and Simon leapt off them, ran to the door, and raced into the passage as fast as their legs would take them. The pixie followed, and even as they all reached the door they saw the wizard and witches landing in the room on their toadstools.

They tore along the passage and up the steps, with the wizard and witches after them. When they got outside they banged the trap-door down, but the wizard pushed it open almost at once. Then the pixie gave a shout of triumph.

'What a silly I am! I'd forgotten I'd got Too-Tall's enchanted stick!' she cried. 'I'll soon settle him!'

She waited till Too-Tall and the witches had climbed out of the trap-door, and then she danced towards them, waving her stick and chanting a long string of words.

The wizard gave a howl of fright, and raced back to the trap-door. The witches followed, and soon there was a bang as the trap-door closed.

'They're gone, and they won't come back in a hurry!' said the pixie, in delight. 'What a good thing I remembered I had Too-Tall's stick. I can use it on Bimbo too, and change him back from a mouse to a cat.'

They all hurried to the pixie's cottage. She drew a circle of chalk on the floor, put the frightened mouse in the middle, waved the enchanted stick and cried out a magic word. Immediately the mouse vanished, and in its place appeared Bimbo, the big black cat!

Bimbo gave a loud purr and leapt over to the delighted children. What a fuss he made of them! They stroked him and loved him and he rubbed his big head against them.

'Now what about a hot cup of cocoa and a slice of cake?' asked the pixie. 'It's quite time you went home, you know, or your mother will be very worried about you.'

So they all sat down to hot cocoa and slices of gingercake. Then the pixie showed them the way home through the wood. She shook hands with them, stroked Bimbo and said good-bye.

'Good-bye,' said Jenny and Simon, 'and thank you ever so much for helping us. We only wish we could do something in return for your kindness.'

'Don't forget I've got the wizard's magic stick!' said the little pixie with a laugh. 'I never in all my life expected to have such a wonderful thing as that! That's quite enough reward for me! Now good-bye to you both, and run home quickly.'

Off went Jenny, Simon and Bimbo, and very soon they ran up the path to their house. Mummy was looking for them, and was getting very anxious. When she heard their story she looked most astonished.

'What an extraordinary thing!' she cried. 'I can hardly believe it, my dears.'

'Well, Mummy, we'll get Bimbo to guide us to the pixie's cottage in Hallo Wood tomorrow,' said Jenny. So the next day they told Bimbo to take them there – but wasn't it a pity, he couldn't remember the way!

'Perhaps he will one day,' said Simon. 'We must wait for that.'

And as far as I know, they are still waiting.

The
Very Little Hen

THERE was once a fine fat hen called Chucky, who laid beautiful brown eggs every single day. She belonged to Dame See-Saw, and was one of a big flock, for the old dame made her living by selling eggs.

Now one day Chucky wandered out of the old woman's garden. She knew she ought not to do this, for she had often been warned that the world outside was not good for hens. But the gate was open and out she walked.

She hadn't gone very far before she met Ten-Toes the pixie.

'Good morning,' he said. 'Come here, my dear, and let me see what sort of an egg you can lay me for my dinner. I'm very hungry indeed, and a nice boiled egg would do me a lot of good!'

So Chucky laid him an egg. It was one of her very best, big and brown, and Ten-Toes was very pleased. He made himself a fire, put his little saucepan on to boil, and very soon the egg

was in the bubbling water. Ten-Toes ate it with a crust of bread, and said that it was the nicest he had ever tasted.

'You must come home with me,' he said to Chucky. 'I'd like an egg like that every day.'

'Oh, I can't come with you,' said Chucky, frightened. 'I belong to Dame See-Saw. I must go back.'

'No, no,' said Ten-Toes, and he picked up the fat brown hen. But she struggled so hard, and pecked his finger so badly that he grew angry.

'Ho ho!' he said, in a nasty voice. 'So you think you won't come with me, do you? Well, I'll soon show you that you're wrong.'

With that he tapped Chucky on the head with his wand and said two magic words. In a trice the hen grew much, much smaller – so small that she was no bigger than a buttercup flower!

'Ha!' said Ten-Toes. 'Now you can peck all you like, but you won't be able to hurt me! And when I get you home, I'll change you back to your right size again, and make you lay me an egg every day!'

But when Chucky heard that, she fled off between the blades of grass, clucking loudly in fear. At first she didn't know what had happened to her, but soon she guessed that she had been made very, very small, for the grass towered above her, and the face of a daisy seemed as big as the sun!

She made her way back to Dame See-Saw and told her all that had happened.

But Dame See-Saw was cross. 'What use are you to me now, I'd like to know!' she cried. 'I can't turn you back to your right size again, and all the other hens will peck you. The eggs you lay will be so tiny that I shan't be able to see them. You can just walk out of the garden gate again, and go to seek your living somewhere else!'

Poor Chucky! She ran out of the gate, clucking in despair. Who would have her, now that she was so small?

'I'll go to Tweedle the Gnome,' she thought. 'He isn't very big. Perhaps he'd like to keep me.'

But Tweedle laughed when he saw Chucky.

'What good would your eggs be to me?' he asked. 'Why, I could put twenty in my mouth at once and not know they were there! No, I don't want you, Chucky.'

Then the little hen went to the goblins in the hill, though she was really rather afraid of them. But they didn't like eggs.

'We never eat them,' they said. 'And we couldn't sell them, Chucky, because they are so very tiny. No, we don't want you, Chucky.

Chucky wandered off to the Wise Man, and begged him to keep her, and she would lay him eggs every day.

'But what could I do with them?' asked the Wise Man. 'They're so small that I should have to put on my biggest pair of spectacles to see them. No, Chucky, I don't want you!'

Poor Chucky went away sadly. Nobody wanted her. There wasn't any room for her anywhere. She went on and on until at last she came to a beautiful garden. In one corner of it was built a play-house for the children, and in this they kept all their toys.

There was a rocking-horse, a big shelf full of books, a toy fort, a Noah's ark, two dolls, a toy clown, a teddy-bear, a box of tricks and last of all, a lovely toy farm. The little hen peeped in at the door and thought it was a fine place. She wondered if there was anyone there who would like to have her for their own.

But Peter and Jane, who owned the lovely play-house, were not there. They were staying at their Granny's, so the toys were all alone.

They saw the tiny hen at the door and called to her to come in.

'What a little mite!' they cried. 'Are you alive or are you a toy like us?'

'I'm alive,' said Chucky, and she told the toys her story, and how she could find nowhere to live. Then the toys all began to talk at once, and there was a tremendous noise. At last the teddy-bear held up his hand for silence, and everyone was still.

'Chucky,' said the teddy-bear to the tiny hen, 'would you like to come and live with us here?

98

There is a toy farm over there, with sheep, cows, horses, goats, pigs, ducks and one cock. There used to be a hen, too, but she got broken. The cock that is left is lonely, and as he is just about your size, we are sure he would be delighted to welcome you to his little shed.'

Chucky was so happy that she could hardly speak. She looked at the little toy farm and thought it was the prettiest place she had ever seen. It was all fenced round, and the farm stood in the middle with the barns and sheds here and there. The farmer and his wife, both made of wood, waved to Chucky.

She ran to them, and they bent down and stroked her. She was just the right size for them. Then the little wooden cock strutted up, and admired Chucky. His feathers were only painted on, but Chucky's were real, and he thought she was wonderful.

'Welcome to my shed!' he said, and he led Chucky to the door of a tiny shed near by.

'I think I'll lay the farmer an egg to show how grateful I am,' said Chucky, and she straight-away laid a beautiful brown egg in the little nesting box there. How delighted the farmer and his wife were! All the toys crowded round to see it, too!

'Well, the other hen that got broken never laid an egg in her life!' cried the farmer's wife. 'What a clever little thing you are, to be sure!'

'Let's have some baby chickens!' cried the farmer. 'We won't eat your eggs yet, Chucky. Lay a dozen in the nesting box, and then sit on them. It would be grand to have twelve yellow chicks running about the farm!'

So Chucky laid twelve brown eggs, and sat on them – and do you know, one morning they all hatched out into the tiniest, prettiest yellow chicks you ever saw! Chucky and everyone else were so proud of them! It made the toy farm seem quite real, to have the little chicks running about everywhere.

Tomorrow Peter and Jane are coming back from their Granny's – and whatever will they say when they see the little chicks, each no bigger than a pea, racing about the toy farm, cheeping loudly? I really can't think!

As for Chucky, she has quite forgotten what it was like to be a great big hen. She is happy as the day is long, trotting about with her chicks on the little toy farm.

The Brave
Little Puppy

ONE day, when Martin and Clare were walking home from school, they saw a man throw a little puppy into a pond, and then run off and leave it.

'Oh!' cried Clare in a rage. 'Look, he's tied a brick round the poor little thing's neck, Martin, and he meant to drown it. Quick! Let's get it out!'

Martin took off his shoes and socks, waded into the pond and picked up the struggling puppy. He quickly undid the string that tied the brick round its neck, and then carried the shivering little creature back to the bank.

'Let's take it home, and see if Mummy will let us keep it,' said Clare. 'Poor little thing! What a horrid man that was!'

They carried the puppy home – but, oh dear, Mummy wouldn't let them have it.

'No,' she said, 'you have two rabbits and a kitten and that's quite enough. You can't have a puppy too. Besides, it is a very ugly little thing.'

'But what shall we do with it?' asked Clare.

'Daddy's got to go to town this afternoon and he'll take it to the Dog's Home,' said Mummy. 'It will be looked after there until someone comes and offers to give it a good home. You had better go with Daddy into town, too, and have your hair cut, both of you.'

So that afternoon Daddy and the two children got into a little brown car and drove off to town. Clare carried the puppy, which wriggled and licked her happily, thinking it had found a lovely master and mistress at last. The children thought it was the nicest little puppy they had ever seen, and even Daddy said it wasn't a bad little thing when it had licked the back of his ear a dozen times.

'Here's the hairdresser's,' said Daddy, pulling up by the kerb. 'Come on, you two. Leave the puppy in the car, and we'll all go and have our hair cut.'

So into the shop they went, leaving the puppy in the car. Soon all three were sitting in chairs with big white cloths round them, and snip, snip, snip went the scissors.

Outside the shop were two men. They had

seen Daddy and the children go into the hairdresser's and they knew that it would be some time before they came out again.

'Let's take this car, Bill,' said one of the men. 'We can jump into it and drive off before anyone stops us!'

'But isn't that a dog inside?' said the other man.

'Pooh, that's only a puppy!' said the first man. 'Come on, quick, before a policeman comes!'

He opened the car door, and at the same moment the puppy started barking his very loudest, for he knew quite well that the two men were not the kind children, nor their father. The man cuffed the puppy, and he bared his little white teeth and snarled. He was very much afraid of this nasty rough man, but the car was in his charge, and he was going to guard it as best he could.

So he flew at the man who was trying to sit in the driver's seat, and bit him in the arm with all his might. The man tore him away and flung him into the back of the car, but, still barking, the brave little dog once more hurled himself at the thief.

Then Martin and Clare heard him barking, and Martin ran to the window and looked out.

'Daddy, Daddy!' he cried. 'There's two men trying to take the car! Quick! Quick! The puppy is trying to stop them, but they'll soon be away!'

Daddy rushed out of the shop at once, followed by the hairdresser and another man. In a trice they had captured the two thieves and the hairdresser went to telephone the police. In a few minutes the bad men were marched off to the police station, and Daddy and the children went back to have their hair finished.

'Well, that puppy is about the bravest little thing I ever saw!' said Daddy. 'I've a good mind to keep him, after this. He stopped our car from being stolen, there's no doubt of that. What about taking him home again, children, and telling Mummy what he's done? Perhaps she would let you keep him then.'

'Oh, Daddy!' cried Martin and Clare in delight. 'Do let's!'

So they all drove home again with the puppy, and Daddy told Mummy how his bravery had saved their car from being stolen. The puppy looked at Mummy with his brown eyes, and wagged his stumpy tail hopefully.

'Well, we'll keep him!' said Mummy. 'I'm sure he will grow up into a very brave, faithful dog. You shall have him, children.'

So that is how Pickles the puppy came to belong to Martin and Clare. He is a grown-up dog now, and twice he has scared away burglars, and once he pulled Baby out of the water when she fell in. Mummy is very glad she let Martin and Clare keep him – and of course they think he is the very best dog in all the world!

The Enchanted Sea

ONE lovely sunny morning John and Lucy went out to play in their garden. It was a very big one, and at the end was a broad field.

'Let's go and play in the field this morning!' said Lucy. So down the garden they ran and opened the gate in the wall, meaning to run out into the green field.

But oh, what a surprise! There was no field there! Instead there was the blue sea – and how Lucy and John stared and stared!

'Lucy! What's happened?' asked John, rubbing his eyes. 'Yesterday our field was here. Today there's a big sea!'

'We must be dreaming,' said Lucy. 'Let's pinch each other, John, and if we each feel the pinch, we'll know we're not dreaming.'

So they each pinched one another hard.

'Ooh!' they both cried. 'Stop! You're hurting!'

'It's not a dream, it's real,' said John, rubbing

his arm. 'But oh, Lucy! It must be magic or something. Let's go and tell Mummy.'

They were just going to run back to the house when Lucy pointed to something on the smooth blue water.

'Look!' she said. 'There's a boat coming – but isn't it a funny one!'

John looked. Yes, sure enough, it was a boat, a very strange one. It had high pointed ends, and at one end was a cat's head in wood and at the other a dog's head. A yellow sail billowed out in the wind.

'Who's in the boat?' said John. 'It looks to me like a brownie or gnome, Lucy.'

'I feel a bit frightened,' said Lucy. 'Let's hide behind our garden wall, John, and peep over the top where the pear tree is.'

They ran behind the wall, climbed the pear tree and then, hidden in its leafy branches, peeped over the top. They saw the boat come nearer and nearer, and at last it reached the shore. Out jumped the brownie, threw a rope round a wooden post near by, and then ran off into the wood to the left of the children's garden.

'Well, that was one of the fairy folk for certain!' said John, in excitement. 'Did you see his pointed hat and shoes and his long beard, Lucy?'

For a long time the children watched, but the little gnome did not come back. After a bit John began to long to see the boat more closely, so he and Lucy climbed down the pear tree and ran quietly over the grass to where the boat lay rocking gently.

'Oh, Lucy, it must be a magic one!' said John. 'Do let's get in it just for a moment to see what it feels like! Think how grand it will be to tell everyone we have sat in a brownie's boat!'

So the two children clambered into the little boat and sat down on the wooden seat in the middle. And then a dreadful thing happened!

The rope round the post suddenly uncoiled itself and slipped into the boat. The wind blew hard and the yellow sail billowed out. The boat rocked from end to end, and off it went over the strange enchanted sea!

'Ooh!' said Lucy, frightened. 'John! What shall we do? The boat's sailing away with us!'

But John could do nothing. The wind blew them steadily over the water, and their garden wall grew smaller and smaller, the farther away they sailed.

'That brownie will be cross to find his boat gone,' said Lucy, almost crying. 'Where do you suppose it's taking us?'

On and on went the little boat, the dog's head pointing forwards and the cat's head backwards. Lucy looked at the back of the dog's head, and thought that it looked a little like their dog at home.

'I do wish we had our dear Rover with us,' she said. 'I'm sure he would be a great help.'

To her great surprise the wooden dog's head pricked up its ears and the head turned round and looked at her.

'If you are fond of dogs, I shall be pleased to help you,' it said.

'You did give us a fright!' said John, almost falling off his seat in surprise. 'Are you magic?'

'Yes, and so is the wooden cat over there,' said the dog. 'We're only wooden figure-heads, but there's plenty of good magic about us. You look nice little children, and if you are fond of animals and kind to them, the cat and I will be very glad to help you.'

'Meeow!' said the cat's head, and it turned round and smiled at the two astonished children.

'Well, first of all, can you tell us about this strange sea?' asked John. 'It's never been here before.'

'Oh yes, it has, but usually at night-time when nobody is about to see it,' said the dog. 'It belongs to the Wizard High-Hat. He sent his servant, the brownie Tick-a-tock, to fetch a red-and-yellow toadstool from the wood near your garden and made the sea stretch from his island to there, so that Tick-a-tock could sail quickly there and back.'

'But I expect he lay down and fell asleep,' said the cat. 'He's always doing that. So when you got into the boat, it sailed off with you instead of the brownie. It doesn't know the difference between you, you see.'

'Oh goodness!' said John, in a fright. 'Does that mean it's taking us to the Wizard High-Hat?'

'Yes,' said the dog, 'and he'll be in a fine temper when he sees you instead of the brownie!'

'Whatever shall we do?' said Lucy, looking anxiously round to see if the wizard's island was anywhere in sight.

'Well, we might be able to help you, if you'll just say a spell over us to make us come properly alive when we get to the island,' said the dog. 'If we were a proper dog and cat we could perhaps protect you.'

'What is the spell?' asked John.

'One of you must stroke my head, and the

other must pat the cat's head,' said the dog, looking quite excited. The cat mewed loudly and blinked her green eyes. 'Then you must say the magic word I'll whisper into your ear, and stamp seven times on the bottom of the boat. Then you'll see what happens when we reach the shore. Don't do any of these things till we reach the island.'

The dog whispered the magic word into each child's ear, and they repeated it again and again to themselves to make sure they had it right. Then suddenly Lucy pointed in front of the boat.

'Look!' she said. 'There's the island – and, oh my! Is that the wizard's palace on that hill in the middle?'

'Yes,' said the dog. 'You'll see some of his soldiers in a minute. They always meet the boat.'

Sure enough the children saw six little soldiers come marching out of the palace gates towards the shore. They were dressed in red, and looked very like John's wooden soldiers at home.

The boat sailed nearer and nearer to the shore, and the dog told John and Lucy to use the spell he had taught them. So John stroked the dog's head, Lucy patted the cat's head, and each of

them said the magic word, and then stamped
loudly on the bottom of the boat seven times.

And what a surprise they had! Each wooden
head grew legs and a body, and hey presto, a
live cat and dog jumped down from the ends
of the boat and frisked round the children in
delight!

'We're real, we're real!' they cried. 'Now we
can go with you and help you.'

The boat grounded on the sandy shore and
the rope flew out and tied itself round a post.
The chief of the soldiers stepped up and looked
most astonished to see the two children.

'Where's Tick-a-tock the brownie?' he asked,
sternly. 'What are you doing here?'

'Well, you see, we stepped into the brownie's
boat and it sailed off with us,' said John. 'We're
very sorry, and please would you ask the wizard
to excuse us and send the boat back to our
garden to take us home again?'

'You must come and ask him yourself,' said
the soldier. 'You are very naughty children!'

The six soldiers surrounded John and Lucy
and marched them off towards the palace on the
hill. The dog and cat followed behind, and the
soldiers took no notice of them.

Soon the children were mounting the long

flight of steps up to the castle, and were pushed into a large hall, where sat the Wizard High-Hat on a silver throne. He looked most surprised when he saw John and Lucy, and at once demanded to know how they got there.

John told him, and he frowned.

'Now that is most annoying,' he said crossly. 'I want to send my sea to another place tomorrow, and that means that Tick-a-tock won't get back with the toadstool. I shall keep you prisoner here for a hundred years, unless you can do the things I tell you to do.'

Lucy began to cry, and John turned pale.

'Please don't set us very hard tasks,' he said. 'I'm only eight years old, and Lucy's only seven, and doesn't know her six times table yet.'

The wizard laughed scornfully, and commanded his soldiers to take the children to the bead-room. They were led to a small room with a tiny window set high up. On the floor were thousands and thousands of beads of all colours and sizes.

'Now,' said the wizard, 'your first task is to sort out all these beads into their different colours and sizes. You can have today and tonight to do this in, and if you haven't finished by tomorrow morning you shall be my prisoners for a hundred years.'

With that he closed the door with a bang, and he and his soldiers tramped away. The children looked at one another in dismay.

'We can never do that!' said Lucy, in despair. 'Why, it would take us weeks to sort out all these beads!'

'Where are the cat and dog?' asked John, looking all round. 'They don't seem to be here. They might have helped us.'

Suddenly the door opened again, and the dog and cat were flung into the room, panting. Then the door closed again, and the four were prisoners.

'We thought we wouldn't be able to get to you!' said the dog. 'So I bit a soldier on the leg and the cat scratched another on the hand, and they were so angry that they threw us in here with you!'

'Just see what we've got to do!' said Lucy, in despair, and she pointed to the beads. 'We've got to sort out all these before tomorrow morning.'

'My word!' said the dog, blowing out his whiskered cheeks. 'That's a dreadful job! Come, Puss! Let's all set to work.'

The four began to sort out the beads, and for an hour they worked steadily. Then the door opened and a soldier put a loaf of bread, a bone, a jug of water and a saucer of milk into the room. Then the door shut and the key was turned.

The children ate the bread and drank the water. The dog gnawed the bone and the cat drank the milk.

'It's no use going on with these beads,' said the cat, suddenly. 'We shall never get them done. I know what I'll do!'

'What?' asked the children, excitedly.

'You wait and see!' said the cat, and she finished her milk. Then she washed herself. After that she went round the little room, and looked very hard at every hole in the wall.

'Now watch!' she said. She sat down in the middle of the floor and began to make a curious squeaking noise that sounded like a thousand mice squealing at once – and a very curious thing happened!

Out of the mouse holes round the room there came running hundreds of little brown mice. They scampered to where the cat sat, and made ring after ring round her. When about a thousand mice were there, the cat stopped making the curious noise and glared at the mice.

'I could eat you all!' she said, in a frightening voice. 'But if you will do something for me, I will set you free!'

She pointed to the beads. 'Sort those out into their different colours and sizes!' she said. 'And be quick about it!'

At once the thousand mice scuttled to the beads. Each mouse chose a bead of a certain colour and size and carefully put it to start a pile. Soon the little piles grew and grew, and the big pile sank to nothing. In half an hour all the thousands of beads were neatly sorted out into hundreds of piles of beads, all of different colours and sizes.

'Good!' said the cat to the trembling mice. 'You may go!'

Off scampered the mice to their holes and disappeared. The children hugged the clever cat, and thanked her.

'Now we'll let the wizard know his task is done!' said the cat. 'Kick the door, John.'

John kicked the door and an angry soldier opened it.

'Tell the wizard we've finished our work,' said John, and the soldier gaped in astonishment to see the neat piles of beads. He fetched the wizard, who could hardly believe his eyes.

'Take them to the Long Field!' said High-Hat to his soldiers. So the children, followed by the cat and dog, were taken to a great field which was surrounded on all sides by high fences. The grass in this field was very long, almost up to the children's knees.

'Here is a pair of scissors for each of you,' said the wizard, with a cunning smile. 'Cut this grass for me before morning, or I will keep you prisoner for a hundred years!'

The children looked at the scissors in dismay. They were very small, and the grass was so long and there was such a lot of it! The wizard and his soldiers shut the gate of the field and left the four alone together.

'Well, I don't know what we're going to do this time!' said John, beginning to cut the grass with his scissors, 'but it seems to me we're beaten!'

He and Lucy cut away for about an hour, but at the end of that time their hands were so tired, and they had cut so small a patch of grass that they knew it was of no use going on. They would never even get a tenth of the field cut by the morning.

'Can't you think of something clever to help us again?' asked John at last, turning to the cat and dog.

'We're both thinking hard,' said the cat. 'I believe the dog has an idea. Don't disturb him for a minute.'

The dog was lying down, frowning. Lucy and John kept very quiet. Suddenly the dog jumped up and ran to Lucy.

'Feel round my collar,' he said to her. 'You'll find a little wooden whistle there.'

Lucy soon found the whistle, and the dog put it into his mouth. Then he began to whistle very softly. The sound was like the wind in the grass, the drone of bees and the tinkling of faraway water.

Suddenly, holes appeared in the earth all around the high fence, and hundreds of grey rabbits peeped out of them. They had dug their way into the field under the fence, and as soon as they saw the dog blowing on his magic whistle, they ran up to him and sat down in rings round him. He took the whistle from his mouth and looked at them.

'I chase rabbits!' he said. 'But I will let you go free if you will do something for me. Do you see this beautiful green juicy grass? Eat it as quickly as you can, and you shall go the way you came.'

At once the rabbits set to work nibbling the green grass. It was very delicious and they enjoyed it. In an hour's time the whole field was as smooth as velvet, and not a blade of grass was longer than Lucy's little finger.

'Good!' said the dog to the rabbits. 'You may go!'

At once they scampered away. John ran to the gate in the fence and hammered on it. The wizard himself opened it, and when he saw the smooth field, with all the long grass gone, he gasped in astonishment.

'Where's the grass you cut?' he asked at last, looking here and there.

The children didn't know what to say, so they didn't answer. The wizard grew angry, and called his soldiers.

'Take them to the top most room of my palace and lock them in!' he roared. 'They have been using magic! Well, they'll find themselves somewhere they can't use magic now!'

In half a minute the soldiers surrounded the children and animals again and hustled them back to the palace. Up hundreds and hundreds of stairs they took them, and at last, right at the very top, they came to a room that was locked. The wizard took a key from his girdle and unlocked the door. The children and animals were pushed inside and the door was locked on the outside.

By this time it was almost night-time. A tiny lamp burnt high up in the ceiling. There was one window, but it was barred across. John looked round in despair.

'Well, I don't see what we can do now!' he said, with a sigh. 'I'm afraid, cat and dog, that even you, clever though you are, can't do anything to help us.'

The dog and cat prowled all round the room, but the walls were strong and thick, and the door was locked fast. For a long time the four sat on the floor together, then suddenly the cat jumped up and ran to the window.

'Open it!' she said. 'I want to see if I can squeeze through the bars.'

Lucy and John opened the heavy window, and the cat jumped lightly on to the ledge.

'What's the good of squeezing through the bars?' asked John, peering down. 'You could never jump down, Puss! Why, we're right at the very top of the palace!'

The cat squeezed through the bars and stood

on the outer window ledge. Her green eyes shone in the darkness.

'There's another window ledge near by!' she whispered. 'I will jump on to that, and see if the window there is open. If it is, I'll go in, and see if I can find some ways of helping you all to escape!'

With that she jumped neatly to the next window ledge, and disappeared. The window there was open and the brave cat leapt lightly into the room. The palace was in darkness. Wizard, soldiers and servants were all sleeping. The soft-footed cat ran down the stairs, and at last reached a room from which loud snores came. She ran in, and by the light of a small candle saw the wizard asleep on his bed. On the table near the candle lay his keys!

In a trice the cat had them in her mouth and back she went up the stairs, leapt on to the window ledge, and then jumped on to the next ledge, mewing to the children as she jumped. How excited they were to see the keys!

John fitted them one by one into the lock of the door until he found the right one. He turned it, and the door opened! Quietly the two children, the cat and the dog slipped down the hundreds of stairs and undid the heavy palace door. Out they went into the moonlight, and ran down to the seashore.

'I do hope the sea still stretches to our garden wall,' said John. 'Hurry up, little boat, and take us home again.'

The boat set off over the water. Suddenly Lucy gave a cry and pointed to each end of the boat. The dog and cat had disappeared, and once more the two wooden figure-heads stood high at each end.

'The magic is gone from them!' said Lucy. 'Oh, I do hope they don't mind. They're gone back to wooden heads again.'

'Don't worry about us,' said the dog. 'We've enjoyed our adventure, and we're quite happy. I only hope the boat will take you home again.'

On and on sailed the little ship in the bright moonlight. After a long time John caught Lucy's arm and pointed.

'Our garden wall!' he said, in delight.

'Who's that on the edge of the sea?' asked Lucy, seeing a little figure standing there.

'It must be Tick-a-tock the brownie!' said John. 'How pleased he will be to see his boat coming back again. I expect he thought he was quite lost.'

The boat touched the grass, and the children

jumped out. They called good-bye to the dog and cat, and then felt themselves pushed aside. The brownie had rushed up to his boat, and leapt in as quickly as he could. The sails filled out and off went the boat in the moonlight, the dog barking and the cat mewing in farewell.

'That's the end of a most exciting adventure,' said John. 'Goodness, I wonder what Mummy has been thinking all this time! We'll tell her all about our adventure, and in the morning perhaps Daddy will make us a raft and we can all go exploring on the magic sea.'

Mummy was glad to see them. She had been so worried. She could hardly believe her ears when she heard all that had happened.

'You must go to bed now,' she said. 'But tomorrow we'll all go down to see the enchanted water, and perhaps Daddy will sail off to the wizard's island to punish him for keeping you prisoner.'

But in the morning the sea was gone! Not a single sign of it was left – there were only green fields and hills stretching far away into the distance. The wizard had called his sea back again, and although John and Lucy have watched for it to return every single day, it never has. Isn't it a pity?

The Goldfish
that Grew

HOPPETTY had a goldfish in a glass bowl, the prettiest little thing you could wish to see, and the pixie was very proud of it indeed. But what puzzled him was that it didn't grow! It kept as small as could be, and Hoppetty became quite worried about it.

'I give it plenty of good food,' he said, 'and it has a nice piece of green water-weed in the globe, and a little black water-snail for company. I do wonder why it doesn't grow.'

But nobody could tell him why.

'Perhaps it isn't very happy,' said Mrs Biscuit, the baker's wife. 'I've heard it said that unhappy creatures never grow much.'

Hoppetty couldn't bear to think that.

'I'm very kind to it,' he thought. 'It ought to be happy. How dreadful if people should think it doesn't grow because I'm unkind to it and make it unhappy!'

He gave the fish more food than ever, but it

wouldn't eat it. The water-snail feasted on it instead, and that made Hoppetty cross. He really didn't know what to do!

Then one day, as he walked over Bumble-Bee Common, he saw a pointed hat sticking up among the gorse bushes, and he knew a witch was somewhere near by. Hoppetty peeped to see.

Yes, sure enough a witch was there, sitting on the ground beside a little fire she had made. On it she had placed a kettle, which was boiling merrily. Soon she took it off, and held over the flames a little fish she had caught in the river near by. She meant to have it for her dinner.

The fish was very small and the witch was hungry.

'I could eat a much bigger fish than you!' Hoppetty heard her say to the little dead trout. 'I think I'll make you bigger, and then I shall have a fine meal!'

She laid the fish down on the grass, and waved her hand over it twice. 'Little fish, bigger grow, I shall like you better so!' she chanted, and then said a very magic word that made Hoppetty shiver and shake, it was so full of enchantment. But goodness! How he stared to see what happened next! The little fish began to grow and grow, and presently the witch took it up and held it once more over the flames, smiling to see what a fine meal she had!

A great idea came to Hoppetty. He would run straight home, and say the spell over his little goldfish! Then it really would grow, and everyone would be so surprised.

Off went Hoppetty, never stopping to think that it was wrong to peep and pry and use someone else's spell when they did not know he had heard it. He didn't stop running till he got home, and then he went straight to his little goldfish swimming about in its globe.

He waved his hand over it twice. 'Little fish, bigger grow, I shall like you better so!' he chanted, and then he said the very magic word, though it made him shiver and shake to do so.

All at once the goldfish gave a little leap in the water, and began to grow! How it grew! Hoppetty couldn't believe his eyes! It was soon twice as big as before, and still it went on growing!

'You're big enough now, little fish,' said Hoppetty. 'You can stop growing.'

But the fish didn't! It went on and on getting bigger and bigger, and soon it was too big for the bowl.

'Oh dear!' said Hoppetty in dismay. 'This is very awkward. I'd better fetch my washing-up bowl and put you in that.'

He popped the fish in his washing-up bowl, but still it went on growing, and Hoppetty had to put it into his bath.

'Please, please stop!' he begged the fish. 'You're far too big, really!'

But the fish went on growing, and soon it was too big for the bath. Then Hoppetty really didn't know what to do.

'I'd better take my fish under my arm and go and find that old witch!' he said at last. 'She can tell me how to stop my goldfish from getting any bigger. Oh dear, I do hope she won't be cross!'

He picked the goldfish up, and wrapped a wet handkerchief round its head so that it wouldn't die, and set off to Bumble-Bee Common. How heavy the fish was! And it kept getting heavier and heavier too, because it went on growing. Hoppetty staggered along the road with it, and everyone stared at him in surprise. Then a gnome policeman tapped him on the arm.

'You are being cruel to that fish,' he said. 'He is panting for breath, poor thing. Put him in that pond over there at once.'

Sure enough the wet handkerchief had slipped off the fish's head, and it was opening and shutting its mouth in despair. It wriggled and struggled, and Hoppetty could hardly hold it. He went to the pond and popped it in. It slid into the water, flicked its great tail and sent a wave right over Hoppetty's feet.

Then who should come by but that witch! Hoppetty ran to her and told her all that had happened, begging her to forgive him for using her spell.

'Do you mean to say that you were peeping and prying on me?' said the witch in a rage. 'Well it just serves you right, you nasty little pixie! Your fish can go on growing till it's bigger than the town itself, and that will be a fine punishment for you!'

'Madam, tell the spell that will make the fish go back to its right size,' said the policeman, sternly. 'Hoppetty has done wrong, but you cannot refuse his request now that he has asked your pardon.'

The witch had to obey. She went to the pond and waved her hand over it twice. 'Big fish, smaller grow, I shall like you better so!' she chanted, and then she said another magic word. At once the great goldfish shrank smaller and smaller, and at last it was its own size again. Hoppetty cried out in delight, and ran to get a net to catch it.

But that little fish wouldn't be caught! It wasn't going to go back into a tiny glass globe again now that it had a whole pond to swim about in, and frogs and stickle-backs, snails and beetles to talk to. Oh no!

Hoppetty had to give it up and he went sadly back home.

'I've lost my little fish,' he said, 'but it serves

me right for peeping and prying. I shan't do that again!'

And I don't believe he ever did!

The Goblin
in the Train

ALL the toys in the playroom were most excited. Tomorrow the clockwork train was going to take them to a pixie party, and what fun that would be.

But, oh dear, wasn't it a shame, when Andrew was playing with the train that day, he overwound it and broke the spring. Then it wouldn't go, and all the toys crowded round it that night, wondering what they would do the next night when they wanted to go to the party.

'I'm very, very sorry,' said the clockwork train. 'But I simply can't move a wheel, you know. My spring is quite broken. You won't be able to go to the pixie party, because I can't take you. It's all Andrew's fault.'

'Well, he must have broken your spring by accident,' said the rag doll. 'He's very careful with us, generally. But it is dreadfully disappointing.'

'Couldn't we send a message to the little

goblin who lives under the holly bush?' said the teddy-bear. 'He is very clever at mending things, and he might be able to mend the broken spring.'

'Good idea!' cried the toys, and they at once sent a message to the goblin. He came in five minutes, and shook his head when he saw the broken spring.

'This will take me a long time to mend,' he said. 'I doubt if I'll get it done by cock-crow.'

'Please, please try!' cried the toys. So he set to work. He had all sorts of weird tools, not a bit like ours, and he worked away as hard as ever he could. And suddenly, just as he had almost finished, a cock crew! That meant that all toys and fairy folk must scuttle away to their own places again, but the little goblin couldn't bear to leave his job unfinished.

'I'll just pop into the cab of the train,' he called to the toys. 'I'll make myself look like a little driver, and as Andrew knows the spring is broken, perhaps he won't look at the train today or notice me. Then I can quickly finish my work tonight and you'll be able to go to the party!'

The toys raced off to their cupboard, thinking how very kind the goblin was. He hopped into the cab, sat down there, and kept quite still, just as if he were a little boy driver.

Andrew didn't once look at his engine that day, and the toys were so glad. When night came again the goblin set to work, and very soon he had finished mending the spring. He wound up the engine, and hey presto, its wheels went round and it raced madly round the playroom.

'Good! Good!' cried the toys. 'Now we can go to the party! Hurrah! What can we do to return your kindness, goblin?'

'Well,' said the goblin, turning rather red, 'there is one thing I'd like. You know, I'm rather an ugly little chap, and I've never been asked to a pixie party in my life. I suppose you wouldn't take me with you? If you could, I'd drive the train, and see that nothing went wrong with it.'

'Of course, of course!' shouted the toys in glee. 'You shall come with us goblin, and we'll tell all the pixies how nice you are!'

Then they all got onto the train, the goblin wound it up again, and they went to the party. What a glorious time they had, and what a hero the goblin was when the toys had finished telling everyone how he had mended the broken train!

He drove them all safely back again to the

playroom and then, dear me, he was so happy and so tired that he fell fast asleep sitting in the cab!

And in the morning Andrew found him there and was so surprised.

'Look, Mummy, look!' he shouted. 'The train has suddenly got a driver, and goodness me, the spring is mended too! Isn't that a strange thing! And isn't he a nice little driver, Mummy? Wherever could he have come from?'

But Mummy couldn't think how he could have got there.

'He must have been there all the time and you didn't notice him before,' she said.

'No, Mummy, really,' said Andrew. 'I've often wished my clockwork train had a driver, and I know I should have noticed him if he had been here before. Oh, I do hope he stays. He looks so nice and real.'

The goblin was so happy to find that Andrew liked him and was pleased with him. But he was happier still that night when all the toys crowded round him and begged him to stay and be one of them.

'We like you very much,' they said. 'Don't go back to your holly bush, but stay here and be the driver of Andrew's train. We'll have such fun together every night!'

The goblin wanted nothing better than to stay where he was, for he had often been very lonely under his holly bush.

'I'd love to stay!' he said. 'Come on, I'll take you for a fine ride round and round the playroom!' The toys almost woke Andrew up with their shouts of delight.

Andrew is very proud of his train-driver. He shows him to everyone, and I do hope you'll see him for yourself some day. Then perhaps you can tell Andrew the story of how he got there.

THE LITTLE GREEN IMP
and other stories

Illustrated by Peter Dennis

Contents

1

Chinky goes adventuring

Chinky was a big, strong brownie who lived in a fine cottage in the middle of Pitpat Village. He had a little friend, a gnome called Dimity, a quiet fellow with a nice smile and neat ways. Dimity thought Chinky a fine brownie and waited on him all day long.

Now Chinky had great ideas of himself. He felt that he had the makings of a hero. If only something would happen so that he could show all the village folk how brave, how full of courage and pluck he was!

'You know, Dimity,' Chinky sometimes said, 'if a house got on fire, I'd be the first one to go and save all the people in it!'

'I'm sure you would, Chinky,' said Dimity admiringly.

'And if a horse ran away I'd be the first one to stop him!' said Chinky.

'There's no doubt about that!' said Dimity, gazing in admiration at tall, strong Chinky.

'And if someone fell into the pond and

couldn't swim I'd jump in straight away and pull him out!' boasted Chinky.

'But I thought you couldn't swim,' said Dimity.

'Oh, that wouldn't matter!' said Chinky. 'I'd be brave enough to jump in all the same.'

'You are so big and strong, Chinky,' said Dimity, with a sigh. 'I'm such a little fellow, and not brave at all. Why, I even run when I see a big spider!'

'You are weak and foolish, Dimity,' said Chinky grandly. 'Never mind – you have a brave friend. If only I could show what a fine chap I am! Nobody seems to think I am anything out of the ordinary. I never have any adventures.'

It was true. Pitpat Village was quiet and well-behaved. No one did anything they shouldn't. Nobody ever had a house on fire. None of the horses ever ran away. Nobody ever fell into the pond or the stream. There were no adventures to be had at all.

So no one knew that Chinky felt so brave. They just nodded to him when they met him, and said 'Good-day!' Or they asked him out to tea and showed him their fine roses or their best sweet-peas and their biggest marrows. It seemed very dull to big, brave Chinky.

'Dimity,' said Chinky, at last, 'I am going to seek adventures. Pack up our things and we will set out tomorrow. If adventures will not come to me, I must go to them.'

So Dimity packed their things into one big bag, put it on his shoulder and set out with his friend. Chinky had long, strong legs and he got along fast. Dimity was always out of breath, for his legs were thin and small, and he had to carry the heavy bag. So he always seemed to be running to catch up.

They walked and they walked. They passed right through Pitpat Village and Chinky shouted to everyone how he was going on brave adventures, and they nodded in surprise.

'You will do something one day, Chinky!' they called, and Chinky marched on, pleased. He left the village behind. He came to farm land, and walked over fields and meadows. And then he came to his first adventure!

'Look!' he cried, stopping and pointing, 'there is something on fire!'

Dimity looked. Yes – smoke was rising up from behind a hedge, and flames crackled loudly.

'It must be a shed or something,' said Chinky. 'Hurry, Dimity, and get a pail for me. There is a stream here, and I will put out the fire. I knew I could be a hero if I had the chance!'

Dimity rushed to a barn not far off, found a

pail, and took it to Chinky. Chinky filled it with water from the stream and threw it on the fire. He got more water and threw it on the flames – and yet more. Soon the fire sizzled loudly, and a cloud of black smoke rose into the air instead of flames and blue smoke.

'The fire is going out,' said Chinky. 'I have put it out!'

Just at that moment there came a roar from behind him. Chinky turned and saw a farmer standing there looking very angry indeed.

'What have you done to my bonfire?' he shouted. 'I was burning up all my rubbish – and now you have interfered and put out the fire! You deserve a good whacking!'

Chinky stared at the angry farmer and then at the fire. Yes – it was a bonfire. He could see that quite plainly now. The farmer lifted up his stick and ran towards Chinky – and the brownie ran away in a terrible fright! Over the fields he ran, and up the hill and down, and he didn't stop till he had lost all his breath. Dimity panted behind him.

Chinky said nothing at all. He didn't feel very brave. Soon he got up and went on again, and it wasn't long before he found his next adventure!

'Look!' he said to Dimity. 'Someone has left their shopping basket behind! They must have put it down for a moment and then forgotten it.

We will find the owner – and how pleased she will be!'

Dimity saw the basket by the hedge, full of bags and parcels. Yes – someone had been shopping – but who? There was no one in sight.

'Shall I carry the basket, Chinky?' Dimity asked.

'Oh, no, I'll carry it,' said Chinky, who was longing to see the owner and have her thanks. He picked it up and set off with it. But he hadn't gone very far before there came an angry yell from the other side of the hedge.

'Stop thief! Stop thief! He's got my basket! I just stepped through the hedge to say good morning to Mrs Flip and someone came along and took my basket! There's the thief! Stop thief! Stop thief!'

A big fat brownie woman came running down the path, red in the face, looking as angry as could be. Behind her came another brownie woman, carrying a rolling-pin.

'Excuse me, madam,' began Chinky politely – but the brownie women did not listen to him. One smacked him on the cheek and the other hit him on the shoulder with her rolling-pin. Poor Chinky! He dropped the basket and fled down the path as fast as ever he could, crying tears all down his nice new coat! He was dreadfully frightened.

Dimity followed with the big bag, panting and puffing, very sorry for his friend.

Chinky dried his tears and went on his way. He felt brave again, ready to go in for any adventure that came, but he did not mean to put out fires nor to pick up baskets. No – he wanted something grander than that!

And he soon found it! He came to a river and saw, in the middle, a boat, rowed by a magician. Sitting in the boat were four pixie-like creatures, with no wings. Just as the boat floated opposite, the magician stopped rowing, took hold of the first pixie and threw him into the water!

'One!' he said. Then he took the second and threw him in as well, 'Two!' Then the third – 'Three!' And then the last. 'Four!' shouted the magician, and stood up in his boat shouting in excitement.

'Look!' said Chinky to Dimity, throwing off his coat. 'Four poor little pixies thrown into the water by that wicked magician! I must rescue them!'

'But you can't swim!' wailed Dimity. Chinky took no notice. He dived into the water and tried to wade out to the pixies – but the water was deep, and, as Dimity had said, Chinky could not swim! So he began to flounder about and shout for help at the top of his voice.

The four pixies, who had been swimming very strongly to the opposite bank, turned at once and made their way to the struggling brownie. They surrounded him and took him to the boat. The magician pulled him in and gazed angrily at him.

'What do you want to get into deep water like this for when you can't swim?' he said. 'I put my four pixies in to have a race, and you have spoilt it all. Silly, interfering creature! I shall take you back with me and make you my servant! Spoiling my plans like this!'

Chinky was dreadfully frightened. He didn't say a word. He didn't like to tell the magician that he had thought he was cruel and had thrown the pixies into the water to drown them. He sat in the boat, shivering and trembling.

Dimity was on the bank, in a terrible way, wondering what was going to happen to Chinky. As the boat was rowed along, he followed it, running on the path. Soon the boat pulled up at a landing-stage, and Dimity saw the magician take hold of poor Chinky very roughly, and haul him up a path and into his house. The four pixies followed. The door slammed. Chinky was a prisoner!

Dimity sat down in dismay. He was very much afraid of magicians. But somehow or other Chinky had got to be rescued. He waited until night had come and everything was dark. Then he crept round to the back of the house and looked in at the window. There, sitting in a corner, with his hands tied, he saw Chinky. No one was with him. Good!

Dimity broke the window with a stone, jumped inside, cut the cords that bound Chinky's hands, and pulled him to the window. At that moment the magician came running in – but Dimity picked up a chair and threw it at him. The magician fell over and yelled in surprise. Before he had picked himself up Chinky and Dimity had disappeared into the night!

And it wasn't *very* long before the two of them were sitting safely and comfortably at home, drinking hot cocoa and grinning shyly at one another. Chinky looked rather red.

'Dimity,' he said, 'I have been foolish. I have found that I am not a hero after all. I don't want to be one, either. I want to stay happily at home with you. But you, Dimity, you are a *real* hero! When I was caught and tied up by the magician, you rescued me, though you must have been very much afraid. You are a brave fellow, Dimity, full of courage. I am proud to have you for a friend!'

Dimity was too happy to speak at first. Then he hugged Chinky and smiled. 'I'm not a hero!' he said. 'I don't want to be one, either. But I love you, Chinky, and so I was brave. But I am not brave really!'

So they had no more adventures, which was just as well, and lived happily together in Pitpat Village – and, unless they have moved, they are still there, to this very day!

2

The Grandpa clock

The Grandpa clock stood up on the landing all day and night, ticking solemnly away by himself. He was a very tall clock, much, much taller than the children, and he was really a grandfather clock, of course – but everyone called him Grandpa because he was so nice.

He didn't like being up on the bedroom landing. He wanted to be down in the hall, and see a bit of life. He wasn't even on the front landing – he was on the back one, where the box room and the guest-room were, so he didn't really see much of anything that went on in the house.

'I wish I was down in the hall!' he thought whenever he heard someone ringing the bell or knocking at the door. 'I wonder who that is? Why can't I be down there and see? And I wish I could go and visit the kitchen. So many people come there. I can hear their voices. The cat goes there a lot too, and I like her.'

But it wasn't a bit of good, the back landing

was his place and there he had to stay. Until one exciting day came – and then things were suddenly quite different!

It happened one night that a small imp called Scuttle-About lost his way in the dark, and climbed in at the landing window to take shelter. He heard the tick-tock, tick-tock of the Grandpa clock, and he ran to it.

'Can I get inside you?' he whispered. 'Will you hide me, Grandpa Clock?'

'Yes! I've a door under my big face. Open it and creep inside,' said Grandpa. 'Be careful of my pendulum that swings to and fro, though. It might hit you.'

The imp was very careful of it. He crouched down below it, and felt it just scrape the top of his head as it swung to and fro. Tick-tock, tick-tock!

He took off his Scuttle-About shoes. They were very magic and he could run about fast as a hare in them – but his feet were tired now and he wanted to curl up and rest for the night.

Soon he was fast asleep and snoring a little. Grandpa ticked steadily all the time, feeling most excited to have a little imp asleep just under his pendulum!

'Tick-tock! It's time to be up! Tick-tock! You must hurry away!' ticked old Grandpa, when he heard the birds beginning to sing outside. He knew that Annie the cook would soon be up and about. He didn't want her to see the imp when he ran off again.

Scuttle-About woke up with a jump. He stretched himself and hit the swinging pendulum with his hand.

'Hey, don't do that!' said Grandpa. 'You'll make me go slow! Hurry – I believe I can hear someone coming.'

The imp swung open the door and fled in a fright. Grandpa never saw him again. But Scuttle-About left something behind him – he left his little magic shoes!

And soon the magic in them spread to the old Grandpa clock. He suddenly felt restless. He ticked a little faster. And then, to his enormous surprise, he gave a little jiggety-jig, rocking to and fro as he ticked.

'Strange! I seem to be able to move!' said Grandpa, astonished. 'I'm sure I moved forward a bit then. There! I did it again. Good gracious – I've moved out from the wall!'

It was the Scuttle-About spell in the little shoes working, of course. But Grandpa didn't know that. He just thought that for some strange reason he could move about.

Move about! Why, he had always longed to do that. He had always wanted to go into the hall and into the kitchen. Suppose he could? Just suppose he could get himself downstairs – how exciting that would be!

Well, it was difficult for him to move very much at first, but he soon got used to it. He could only move by rocking himself, or doing a curious little jump that made him tick very fast indeed as if he were quite out of breath.

It took him quite half an hour to reach the front landing. Even that was exciting to him because it was years since he had seen it. There were flowers there, and a big chair, and a chest. Grandpa ticked away to them in a loud voice: 'I'm going downstairs when I've got my breath! I'm going exploring!'

But he didn't get downstairs because at that moment the children's father came out of his room to go and wake the children. He almost bumped into Grandpa, who was just outside his bedroom door.

'Good gracious! It's the Grandpa clock!' he said. 'However did it get here? Has someone been having a joke?'

Poor Grandpa! He was carried straight back to his own place on the back landing. He was bitterly disappointed. He grumbled away to himself, ticking very crossly.

'Tick-tock, what a nasty shock, for a poor old clock!' he ticked. The children soon heard that he had been found outside their father's door, and they came to stare at him.

'Who put you there? Grandpa, don't you start wandering about at night!' they said.

Well, the Grandpa clock wasn't going to stop his bit of travelling if he could help it! Somehow or other he was going to get downstairs! Surely, if the family found him in the hall they would let him stay there? Wasn't that the proper place for a big grandfather clock?

That afternoon, when the children were at school and their mother was resting, the clock felt it couldn't keep still on the dull back landing any longer. He must at least go to the top of the stairs and look down.

So he went to the top of the stairs, rocking himself slowly along, sometimes giving a funny little jump. He couldn't help feeling very excited.

The stairs looked very long and very steep. It wasn't much good thinking of rocking himself down them. He would have to do jumps down from one stair to the next. Down he went – jump – jump – jump – hop!

It was very dangerous. He nearly missed a stair once or twice, and shivered in fright. But at last he was at the bottom, standing in the hall. How wonderful!

The hall seemed a most exciting place. There were mats and chairs, umbrellas, walking-sticks and a little table with flowers on. Now, where could the clock put himself so that he could see when people came to the door? He badly wanted to have a bit of company.

20

The cat had heard the noise Grandpa made coming downstairs, and she came out of the kitchen to see what it was. She was amazed to see the Grandpa clock standing by the hall-table! She went up and sniffed at it. The sniffing tickled Grandpa, and made him jump.

That frightened the cat. She put her tail in the air and fled to the kitchen. The clock heard voices coming from there.

'I must go there and listen,' he thought, so he rocked and hopped to the kitchen door. The cook was out in the scullery talking to the milkman and the baker. Grandpa rocked inside and stood by the cupboard. My, what a thrilling place the kitchen was – and look at that lovely red fire! Grandpa began to wish he lived in the kitchen.

The cook came back. She saw Grandpa at once and gave a scream. 'Milkman! Baker! Help, help! Here's old Grandpa in the kitchen!'

They came rushing in, expecting to see an old man. Cook pointed to the clock. 'There, look! How did he get here? Oh, oh, I feel faint!'

The Grandpa clock was scared. When the milkman and the baker helped the cook to a chair, he rocked himself out of the kitchen and put himself back in the hall. He stood there, feeling very excited. My word, this was life!

The children's mother came running down the stairs. She suddenly saw Grandpa by the hall table, and stopped in amazement.

'Cook!' she called. 'Why is Grandpa down in the hall!'

'Oh, Mam! Do you mean to say he's there now?' cried the cook, looking into the hall. 'He was standing in the kitchen a minute ago!'

'Oh, nonsense!' said the children's mother. *How* did he get into the hall? This is most extraordinary.'

The children were surprised to hear what had happened when they got home.

The cook told them how Grandpa had appeared in the kitchen, then their mother told them how she had seen him in the hall.

'Perhaps old Grandpa is dull and bored, living up on the back landing, where nothing happens and nobody goes,' said Mary. 'Can't we let him live in the hall? He's so nice.'

But back on the landing he had to go. He was really most annoyed. Now he would have to hop all the way downstairs again if he wanted to stand in the hall.

'I'll wait till night comes and everyone is in bed,' he thought, ticking solemnly on the landing. 'Then I'll go down again, and look into all the rooms. That will be most exciting.'

Now, that night, when it was very dark and everyone was asleep, old Grandpa thought he would go downstairs once more. And at the same moment that he thought this he heard a little noise downstairs. Who was it? The cat wandering about? Or mice playing? Perhaps it was that imp coming back again.

Grandpa decided to go and see. So off he went, rocking himself to the top of the stairs. He stood at the top, and heard a noise again. The noise wasn't the cat, or the mice, or the imp. It was a burglar! He had got into the house and was in the hall. Think of that!

Grandpa hopped down the first stair. Then he hopped down the next one – but alas, he missed! With a really tremendous noise he slid and slithered all the way from the top to the bottom, and landed on the top of the alarmed burglar. He was knocked over like a skittle, and lay on the carpet, quite still.

Then things happened quickly. Doors flew open, lights went on, voices called out. 'What was that noise, what's happening?' And down the stairs poured the whole family.

'Why, my goodness me, here's a man lying flat on the floor and the old Grandpa clock on top of him!' said the children's father in astonishment. 'Ring up the police, quickly!'

The police came. They took the burglar away. One of them nodded at the old clock, which had now been stood upright in the hall,

and was watching everything in the greatest excitement.

'What was your clock doing, knocking burglars down in the middle of the night? Good thing you had him in the hall!'

'Well, we didn't. He lives on the back landing,' said Mary. 'But oh – do, do let him live downstairs in the hall, Daddy, will you? I'm sure he wants to! I'm sure he was coming downstairs and he slipped and fell on top of the burglar. He deserves a reward, Daddy, he really does!'

24

So now old Grandpa lives downstairs, and loves it. And nobody has discovered to this day that he has a tiny pair of Scuttle-About shoes inside his case! It will be sad if somebody takes them out, won't it? He won't ever be able to wander into the kitchen at night and talk to the cat.

Tick-tock, tick-tock. I believe I can hear him coming!

3

Mister Icy-Cold

Once upon a time, one very snowy week, six children began to build a snowman. How hard they worked! You should have seen them, scraping the snow off the grass and off the top of the hedges, slapping it together to make the snowman's body, and patting it neatly into shape.

'This is fun!' said Mary.

'He will be the biggest snowman ever seen!' said Alan.

'I shall ask Mother to give me an old cap of Daddy's for him to wear,' said Eileen.

'Let's give him two feet, and put shoes on them so that he can walk about if he wants to!' said John.

The others laughed. 'I *should* be astonished if I saw him walking down the garden!' said Ian.

'We'll call him Mister Icy-Cold!' said Gillian.

When they had finished the snowman it was

three o'clock. 'Now we will dress him!' said Mary.

'He has a head as big as a giant's football!' said Alan.

'Here's Daddy's old cap for him!' said Eileen, running up with a big checked cap and putting it on the snowman's head. He did look grand!

'And here are two old shoes belonging to Grandpa!' said John, putting them on the snowman's feet. It was difficult to put them on! John filled the shoes with snow, and then pushed them well under the snowman, so that they stuck out in a very real manner!

'He's going to walk, he's going to walk!' cried Ian.

'Come along indoors and have a nice hot drink of milk, Mister Icy-Cold!' shouted Gillian.

'He wouldn't like that,' said Mother, coming up to look at the wonderful snowman. 'It would melt him inside!'

The children went in to tea. When the moon rose up in the sky, just about their bed-time, they looked out of the window and saw Mister Icy-Cold standing out there in the garden looking as real as could be. He wore Daddy's cap, he smoked an old pipe, he had two great black eyes, he wore a ragged scarf round his neck, old gloves on his hands, and Grandpa's shoes. He really looked marvellous.

In the middle of the night a crowd of little snow-elves came flying up in their pretty sleigh, drawn by winter moths. When they saw Mister Icy-Cold they flew down to him at once.

'Oh!' they cried. 'A great big snowman! What is your name, Snowman?'

'I am Mister Icy-Cold,' said the snowman, in a soft snowy sort of voice. 'Come and talk to me.'

The snow-elves told him where they had come from – a land far away to the north, where there was always ice, always frost, always snow. The elves were pretty little creatures with frosty dresses, and wings as soft and as white as snow. Mister Icy-Cold liked them very much indeed. He felt lonely when they had gone. But they promised to come again the next night.

They kept their promise – but to Mister Icy-Cold's great dismay they were crying bitterly!

'What's the matter?' asked Mister Icy-Cold.

'Oh, two naughty pixies chased us, and broke our pretty sleigh. Look! It's no use now! We can't use it any more. We don't know what to do because, when the weather turns warm, we must fly away to our own country of ice and snow. If we stay here when it is warm, we feel ill and fade away.'

Mister Icy-Cold was very sorry to hear all this.

'Where do those two pixies live?' he asked. 'I will go to them and make them mend your sleigh for you, or else give you a new one.'

'But snowmen can't walk!' cried the snow-elves.

'Oh, *can't* they!' said Mister Icy-Cold, and he laughed. 'Look!'

He stepped forward on his two big feet, and the elves cried out in surprise, for they had never seen a snowman walk before. He plodded down the garden and back, his two big shoes leaving footprints behind him.

'There you are!' he said. 'What did I tell you? Now where do those two naughty pixies live? I'll go and give them the fright of their lives!'

'Come with us and we'll show you,' said the elves, and dragging their broken sleigh behind them, they took the snowman down the garden, through a gate at the bottom, and into a field. The field sloped up into a hill, and in the middle of the hill was a little door.

'This is where the pixies live,' said the elves, half-frightened. Mister Icy-Cold knocked at the door softly. As soon as it was opened by the two pixies, the snowman reached out his big gloved hand and caught hold of them.

'Oooh! Ow! Oooh!' yelled the pixies, in a

29

fright. 'He's a big white giant! Oooh! Let us go!'

'You broke the sleigh belonging to the snow-elves!' said the snowman sternly. 'What are you going to do about it?'

'Oh, we'll mend it; oh, do let us go! We promise to mend it!' squealed the pixies. Mister Icy-Cold put them down on the ground, and looked at them sternly out of his big black stone eyes.

'Do it at once, or I'll carry you off with me!' he said. The pixies took the broken sleigh and looked at it. One of them fetched hammer and nails and screws. The other brought a few pieces of wood. Soon the night air was filled with the sound of hammering. Every now and again the two pixies stared round in fear at the big snowman, and he frowned as hard as he could.

'Get on with your job!' he said. So they hurried and hurried. The wind blew chill and Jack Frost was out and about. The pixies were cold and wanted to get back into their warm little house. Soon the sleigh was mended, and the snow-elves got into it with glad shouts and cries.

'Don't you dare to interfere with the snow-elves again,' said Mister Icy-Cold, and off he shuffled back to his place in the garden. The snow-elves went with him, making a great fuss of him, and telling him he was their best friend.

After that the elves and the snowman talked together every night. But soon the weather changed and the air became warm. The snow-elves began to think about going back to their own country of ice and snow.

'But how lonely I shall be without you!' said Mister Icy-Cold sadly. 'I shall stand here, thinking of you, all the spring and summer

through, till the winter comes again and brings you with it.'

'No, Mister Icy-Cold, you won't stay here all the spring and the summer,' said the elves. 'You will melt. You will melt right away, and there will be nothing left of you when we come back next winter.'

Mister Icy-Cold stared at the elves in horror, and his stone eyes seemed to get bigger and bigger.

'Melt!' he said. 'Did you say I shall melt? Won't there be anything left of me?'

'Not a thing,' said the elves sadly. 'That's the worst of being a snowman, you know. You only last whilst the snow and ice are here. Then you disappear for ever.'

Nobody spoke for a minute. Mister Icy-Cold was too upset, and the elves too sad. Then a small elf gave a little squeal that made everybody jump.

'I've got an idea, I've got an idea!' she cried. 'Why shouldn't Mister Icy-Cold come back to our land with us! It's always cold and frosty there, and snow is always on the ground. He would never melt there. He would be able to live with us for ever!'

'Of course, of course!' shouted the snow-elves in delight. 'You must start tonight, Mister Icy-Cold. We will make our winter moths fly very slowly, and you must follow us carefully.

Come now, this very minute – for the weather is getting warmer, and if you begin to melt you may not be able to walk!'

So Mister Icy-Cold followed the little sleigh, drawn by moths, and plodded on and on and on towards the north. He went over fields and hills, down lanes and high roads, and the elves always found a good place to hide him in the daytime.

Once the weather got a bit too warm, and the snowman's nose melted a bit. But the next night was frosty again, so he was all right. And at last he got to the land of the snow-elves. He was safe!

'Welcome to our home!' cried the snow-elves, kissing him on his cold cheek. 'You shall build yourself a little snow-house with windows and a door, and do just whatever you like.'

The six children who had built the snowman were most surprised to find him gone.

'Oh, he's just melted,' said Mother.

'But, Mother, his cap, and his scarf, and his gloves and his shoes can't have melted too!' said Mary. 'It's most mysterious! I wonder where he is, funny old Mister Icy-Cold?'

He was building himself a little house in the land of the snow-elves, as happy as could be! And there he lives to this day, still wearing the same old cap and the same old shoes – funny Mister Icy-Cold!

4

Wisky, Wasky and Weedle

Once upon a time there were three gnomes called Wisky, Wasky and Weedle. Wisky was small, Wasky was tall, and Weedle was fat. They were lazy, mischievous rascals, and they lived in a tiny cottage called Chimneys.

Now one day when Wisky wanted to go out to buy sausages for dinner, he found there was no money at all in the purse they kept on the mantelpiece. He turned it inside out and showed it to the others.

'We've got to do some work, boys,' he said. 'No money, no sausages!'

They sat down on their stools to think hard. Presently Wisky grinned and slapped his knee. 'I've got a fine idea!' he said.

'What?' asked the others.

'We'll borrow Mr Sooty's chimney-brushes,' said Wisky. 'And we'll go to the next town where nobody knows us. I will be the sweep and sweep the chimney; but I'll be sure to make the carpets and everything in a dreadful mess before I go – and that's where *you* come in, Wasky!'

'Go on,' said Wasky.

'You see, as soon as I have left, and the lady is grumbling about the soot all over the place, *you* come up, Wasky, with brooms and dusters and cloths, and say you are a cleaner. So you get the job of going in and cleaning the house.'

'And where do *I* come in?' asked Weedle.

'Well, before Wasky goes, he leaves the taps running,' said naughty Wisky, with a giggle. 'Then, just as the water is running over everywhere and the lady is trying to get a plumber to come in and put things right, *you* come along, Weedle, and say you are a handyman and can do any job like that. You turn off the taps, clear up the mess, take your pay and join us! Now isn't that a fine idea? We each make a job for the other, you see.'

'Come on, then,' said Wasky, getting up. 'You go and borrow Mr Sooty's brushes, Wisky.'

Very soon, with chimney-brushes, ordinary brushes, and dusters and cloths and a bag of tools, the three gnomes went over the hill to Fiddle-dee-dee, the next town. They looked about for a house where the smoke from a chimney was very black, for they knew that perhaps that would want sweeping – and very soon they saw one.

'Look, there's a chimney that wants sweeping!' said Wisky, pointing to it. 'Now I go first, boys.'

Off he went to the back door, carrying his sweep's brushes over his shoulder. He rang the bell. A sharp-faced little brownie-woman came to the door.

'Good morning, madam; your chimney wants sweeping and I'm the man to do it for you,' said Wisky, taking off his cap.

'Are you clean in your work, and quick?' asked the brownie-woman. Wisky said he was – and she led the way indoors and up to a bedroom where a fire was burning. She put it out and told Wisky to sweep the chimney and not make a mess.

Wisky fitted together his chimney-brushes and pushed them up the chimney. He meant to make a fine old mess, of course – but, dear me, he didn't need to try to make one! That chimney was almost choked up with soot, and as soon as Wisky's brush moved it, a great pile of fine black soot fell down the chimney, bounced on the hearth and covered Wisky from top to toe! He began to cough and splutter. The soot flew out into the room and settled everywhere – my, what a mess there was!

Wisky took a look at it. He felt frightened. He hadn't meant to make quite such a mess as

36

that! He stuck his head up the chimney to see if there was any more soot there – and another lot fell all over him!

'I'd better stop this,' thought Wisky. 'I'll put my brushes together and go downstairs and ask for my money. I'm sorry for Wasky! He *will* have a mess to clear up!'

He went downstairs. When the brownie-woman saw him she gave a scream.

'Ooooooh! What are you?'

'I'm the chimney-sweep, madam,' said poor Wisky.

'Well, you want a wash,' said the brownie-woman, and she took hold of Wisky by his hair and popped him just as he was into a tub of hot soapy water she had nearby, ready for her washing. My goodness me! What a shock for Wisky! But that wasn't all. When she had finished washing him she took him out into the garden and pegged him up on the line by his coat-collar to dry. Poor Wisky!

Now Wasky and Weedle were waiting outside, and when Wisky didn't come out, Wasky was cross.

'He's slipped out of the back door with his money and gone home,' said Wasky. 'It's too bad. Well, I'm going in to do my share, Weedle. You'll be next.'

He went and knocked at the door. The brownie-woman opened it, looking worried and upset, for she had just seen the terrible mess in her bedroom.

'Any cleaning you want done, madam?' asked Wasky, showing his brooms and dusters. 'I'm the man for you, if you've got a dirty room you want turned out!'

'Well, it just happens I *do* want someone,' said the brownie-woman. 'I've had a sweep here and he has left the bedroom in such a mess that I really don't know what to do about it. Come in.'

In stepped Wasky and went up to the bedroom, grinning, but when he saw the truly dreadful mess everywhere that Wisky had left, he turned quite pale. What, clean up all that! Good gracious, it would take him hours, and be too much like real hard work! But he had to set to work.

Now Wasky had no real idea how to clean a dirty sooty room, and he set to work to sweep up the soot with his biggest brush – and, of course, the soot flew up into the air and made more mess than ever! Wasky got desperate – he swept and he swept – and the soot flew and flew. It got into his eyes – and his nose – and his mouth – it flew from the bedroom into the bathroom. Wasky made the mess twice as bad, and was quite frightened when he suddenly caught sight of himself in the glass.

'Gracious me!' he said. 'How dreadful I

look! I think I'll just turn on a few taps so that there is a nice watery mess for Weedle to clear up – and then I'll ask for my money and go.'

He turned on all the taps he could see. Then he shut the bathroom door and went downstairs. But before he could even open his mouth to ask for his money, the brownie-woman gave a shriek! 'What! You're as bad as the chimney-sweep!' she cried. 'What a dreadful mess you are in!'

She popped Wasky into a tub of soapy water and soon he too was out on the line, hanging there in the wind beside Wisky! And Weedle waited outside the house, wondering why Wasky didn't come out.

At last he went to the door and rang the bell, just in time to hear the brownie-woman shouting for help.

'Something's gone wrong with the water! The water is pouring down the stairs! Help! Help!'

Weedle went in with his bag of tools. 'Madam, I am a plumber,' he said. 'I will soon put things right for you.'

He rushed upstairs and turned off the taps. My goodness, you should have seen the bathroom! The bath was full and overflowing, and so was the basin. There was water swirling about the floor, running out on to the landing, into the bedroom and down the stairs! What with the black soot everywhere, and the water, there was a fine old muddle!

Suddenly, Weedle slipped and fell – splash! into the water. 'Oooooomph!' he said, as he swallowed a huge mouthful of sooty water. 'Oooooomph! It's down my neck! It's in my boots! It's all over me! Help! Help! I'm drowning! I can't swim!'

He tried to get up but fell over again – and suddenly down the stairs he slid with the pouring water, and landed – ker-plumkity-plunk! – at the bottom. There the brownie-woman stood, with rubber boots on, trying to sweep the water out of the back door.

'Bless us all!' she said, as she caught hold of Weedle by the hair and shook him well. 'Here's another to go on the line.'

And will you believe it, she took Weedle and pegged him up on the line to dry too! There the three gnomes hung in the wind, swinging to and fro, wishing and wishing they had never thought of playing such tricks on anyone!

The brownie-woman swept her house out and dried it. She cleaned away the soot and opened the windows to let the air in. And then she took a carpet-beater and she went to the line where Wisky, Wasky and Weedle hung, and gave them all the hardest spanking they had had in their lives.

'You are three rogues!' she said, as she unpegged them. 'I can see through your tricks. Now go home, and make up your minds to do better – or I'll come and peg you up on my line again, as sure as my name is Dame Slip-Slap.'

Poor Wisky, Wasky and Weedle! I feel sorry for them – but it served them right all the same, didn't it!

5

The cow that lost her moo

There was once a pretty cow called Buttercup. Everyone was very fond of her, for she was a gentle creature, though rather stupid. She lived in a big field with twelve other cows, and she was the prettiest of the lot.

One day she caught a cold and she lost her voice. She tried her hardest to moo loudly just as she had always done – but it wasn't any good at all. Not the tiniest bit of moo came out of her big mouth. Buttercup had no voice except a small whisper that sounded rather like dry leaves rustling together.

'This will never do!' thought Buttercup to herself in a great fright. 'I *must* get some sort of voice. I can't go about whispering. Even the ducks on the pond over there have a louder voice than I have. If I can't moo perhaps I can learn to quack!'

So that night, when the Little Folk came running out in the fields, Buttercup whispered to one of them.

'Pinkity, I've lost my lovely moo. Could you get me another one, do you think? – or at any rate could you get me another voice of some sort? I hate talking in a whisper like this; it is so stupid for a big cow like me to have such a tiny whispery voice.'

Pinkity looked at the great cow and grinned all over his cheeky little face. 'I can't get you a moo,' he said. 'But I could get you a quack, if you like! I know those ducks would spare me one if I asked them.'

Buttercup nodded her head. Off went Pinkity, spoke to the ducks, and then came back with something wrapped up in a dock leaf. 'Here you are,' he said to the grateful cow. 'Swallow this and you'll find you have a fine new voice!'·

So Buttercup swallowed down the dock leaf with the quack spell inside – and at once she found that she could quack! You should have heard her! Really, it was very funny to hear a great cow quacking away for all she was worth. Her friends came round her in surprise.

'Why do you quack?' they asked. 'You are very foolish, Buttercup. The farmer will think you are a duck, and will put you on the pond to swim with the others. You will have to lay eggs for him.'

'Quack, quack!' cried Buttercup, in a great fright. 'I couldn't lay an egg! I know I couldn't!

And I should die of fear if I had to swim on the pond! Pinkity, where are you? Quack, quack, quack! Take away this quack and bring me some other voice. I can't bear it!'

Pinkity hopped up. He was very much enjoying himself. He caught a loud quack as Buttercup spoke, and wrapped it up in another dock leaf. He put it into his pocket, and hurried off. He went to a brown mouse for a little squeak. She gave it to him wrapped up in a daisy leaf, for it was very small.

He ran back to Buttercup and gave it to her. She swallowed it – and then began to squeak in a very high voice, just like the mouse. All the other cows began to moo with laughter.

'Buttercup, how foolish you are!' they said. 'Now you have a voice like a mouse. The weasel will come along when he hears you, and will try to bite you, thinking you are a mouse – and the big owl will pounce down on you.'

'Too-whoo-too-whoo!' called the owl, in the distance. Buttercup began to tremble. She was in a great fright.

'Pinkity, Pinkity!' she squeaked. 'Come here! Take away this squeak, I beg of you, and bring me a better voice. I can't bear this. Squeak, squeak. Eeeeeeee!'

Pinkity took away the squeak and ran off again, beaming. This was a great joke. What a tale to tell when he went home in the morning!

This time he went to a sheep lying down on the hillside, and asked her to lend him her baa. She did so, and he carried it off, wrapped up in two nettle leaves. Buttercup swallowed it gratefully and at once began to baa and bleat in a most sheep-like manner.

All her friends stared at her in amazement. Whatever would she do next?

'Buttercup, are you turning into a sheep?' asked Daisy, a pretty white cow.

'No,' said Buttercup. 'Of course not. I am a cow. Baa-aa! Baa-aa!'

'Well, the farmer will be sure to think you are a sheep if you baa like that,' said Daisy. 'He will expect you to grow wool for him and will clip your coat just as he does those of the sheep. My! You will be cold with all your coat clipped away!'

Buttercup was horrified. What! Have her nice hairy coat clipped away so that she might grow a thick covering of wool? Never! 'Baa, baa, baa!' she bleated to Pinkity. 'Oh, do take this voice away quickly. I can't bear it. Baa, baa!'

Pinkity hopped up and took it away. He gave it back to the surprised sheep, and then hunted round for someone else who might lend him a voice. He met Bobby, the dog, out rabbiting by himself in the moonlight, and he called to him.

'Hi, Bobby! Will you lend me your bark for a little while?'

'No,' said Bobby. 'I want it.'

'Now, listen, Bobby,' said Pinkity. 'I'll show you the best rabbit-hole in the field if you'll lend me your bark for a time. Please do. I'm having such fun with a foolish cow. I've made her quack, squeak and baa. Now I want to make her bark.'

'Well, mine's a very *fierce* sort of bark,' said Bobby. 'She will frighten all the other cows if they hear it. So I warn you, Pinkity . . . you'd really better not borrow it!'

But Pinkity said yes, he really must have it. So Bobby gave it to him, wrapped up in a piece of paper he found in the ditch. Off went Pinkity over the fields to Buttercup. 'Here you are,' he said, giving her the bark in the piece of paper. She ate it up, paper and all.

And then, stars and moon! She began to bark like a very fierce dog!

'Wuff, wuff, wuff! Grrrrrrrrr! Wuff, wuff, wuff, wuff! GRRRRRRRRRRRRRRRR!'

There had been a growl mixed up with the bark, and so Buttercup growled as well as barked. The other cows, who all disliked and feared dogs, were terrified almost out of their lives. They rushed off to the other end of the field in a fright.

As for Buttercup, she was terribly frightened

too! She hated dogs, and this bark and growl she had made her very much afraid. She galloped away – and trod so heavily on Pinkity's toe that he yelled with pain. He limped off crying big tears down his cheeky little face, and went home to bathe his poor foot.

So when Buttercup went to find him to beg him to take her bark away, he was nowhere to be seen! No – he was safely at home, tying up his poor squashed toe in a bandage, wishing very much that he hadn't played such silly tricks on foolish Buttercup!

Buttercup barked all through the night, and growled when she wasn't barking. Her friends were so frightened of her that they wouldn't let her come near them.

'If you come any nearer we will run our horns into you!' they cried. 'You are turning into a dog, there's no doubt! You will have to live in a kennel and eat biscuits and bones, instead of sweet grass.'

Buttercup was very unhappy. She went away into a corner and barked all to herself. 'Why did I bother about my voice?' she thought sadly. 'I would rather have no moo at all than bark like a dog. This is dreadful. What will the farmer say when he milks me?'

The farmer was scared and puzzled when he heard Buttercup's new voice. He stared at her as if he couldn't believe his ears. A cow barking? What next?

'Wuff, wuff!' said Buttercup, hanging her head in shame. 'Wuff, grrrrr!'

'I shall have to sell you, Buttercup,' said the farmer, seeing how frightened of her all the other cows seemed to be. 'I can't have a barking cow.'

'Wuff, grrr!' said Buttercup, most unhappily. She couldn't bear the thought of being sold. It would be dreadful to leave the fields she knew and go somewhere strange.

All that day she barked and growled, and

when night came she looked out anxiously for Pinkity. That rascally little creature had been feeling sorry that he had played such tricks on Buttercup. His toe was very painful, and he thought it must be a punishment for him.

'I'd better go out and see how Buttercup is tonight,' he thought to himself. 'Even though I can hardly walk, I must certainly go.'

So out he went into the field. No sooner had he gone through the gate than he almost jumped out of his skin. He heard what seemed to him to be a very fierce dog barking and growling just above him. Of course, it was Buttercup waiting for him. What a fright he got!

'Wuff, wuff, grrrrr!' said Buttercup. 'Do pray take this terrible voice away, Pinkity. Wuff! I frighten everyone and myself too. I would rather have no voice at all. It was foolish of me to want one.'

Pinkity took the bark and growl away and wrapped them carefully in his handkerchief. Then he limped off to find Bobby, who, he was sure, would be wanting his bark badly.

So he was. He was very angry indeed about it!

'You said you only wanted my bark for a little while!' he scolded. 'Here I've had to be all day without either my bark or my growl and couldn't even bark at an old tramp who came and stole some eggs. Give me my bark at once!'

49

Pinkity gave it to him – and then forgot all about his bad foot, for angry old Bobby chased him up the lane and over the fields, barking at the top of his voice!

'Wuff! You mischievous creature! Grrrrr! You scamp, you rogue! Wuff, grrr, wuff!'

Buttercup was very thankful indeed to have lost her bark. She ate the grass quietly, and when her friends saw that she no longer barked or growled they came round her once again and talked to her.

And suddenly she found herself mooing to them! Yes – her cold had gone away, and she had got her own voice back once more! It had gone only for a little while whilst she had a cold. So she needn't have worried herself so much after all!

'To think I had a quack, a squeak, a baa, a bark and a growl!' said Buttercup to herself, in shame. 'When all the time, if only I'd been patient, my own voice was just waiting to come back. Really, I am a very foolish cow! I do hope the farmer won't sell me now.'

He didn't, of course. When he found that Buttercup was her own self again, and mooed just as she always did, he patted her and said: 'Well, well – I can't think what happened to you yesterday, Buttercup – but you seem all right today, so, as you give me a nice lot of creamy milk, I shan't sell you!'

'Moo, moo, moo!' said Buttercup, and whisked her tail happily. Then she whisked it again and knocked off the farmer's hat. But he didn't seem to mind!

6

Lazy Luke

Once upon a time Lazy Luke fell asleep in front of his fire, and when he woke up it had gone out. He shivered.

'Look at that now – the fire's out and I've no more wood. I'll go and borrow a bundle from Dame Hurry-About.'

So he went across the road to Dame Hurry-About's cottage and asked her for some wood.

'You lazy fellow!' she said. 'Why don't you go to the woods and pick some up – there's plenty there!'

'It's a long way,' said Lazy Luke. 'You just lend me a few sticks, Dame Hurry-About, and I'll bring you plenty tomorrow.'

'Well, you do something for *me* first,' said Dame Hurry-About. 'You go and ask Mr Borrow-A-Lot to let me have back the teapot of mine I lent him yesterday. Then I'll let you have some sticks.'

'Oh bother! He lives up the hill,' said Lazy Luke.

'Well, no teapot, no sticks,' said Dame Hurry-About, so Luke had to go. He walked up the hill to Mr Borrow-A-Lot and saw him sitting down having a cup of tea out of Dame Hurry-About's teapot.

'Dame Hurry-About says, please will you give me her teapot that you borrowed yesterday,' said Lazy Luke.

'Well, as you can see, I'm using it,' said Mr Borrow-A-Lot. 'But I'll be finished in five minutes. You just pop down to Mother Cranky's and ask her if she can spare me a new-laid egg. She said she might have one for me today.'

'Oh *dear*!' said Lazy Luke. 'All that way! No, I'll sit down and wait till you're ready to give me the teapot.'

'Oh no you won't,' said Mr Borrow-A-Lot. 'No new-laid egg, no teapot!'

So Lazy Luke went off to Mother Cranky's, and he had to knock at her door four times before she opened it.

'Now, now, now, who's this waking me up out of my nap!' she said crossly. 'Oh, it's you, Lazy Luke. What do you want?'

'Mr Borrow-A-Lot says you promised him a new-laid egg today,' said Lazy Luke. 'I've come to get it for him.'

'Well, fancy you putting yourself out to do a job for anyone!' said Mother Cranky. 'That does surprise me! I'll have to go and look in my hen-house to see if there's an egg there. You do something for me while I'm looking. Pop over to Father Hoo-Ha's and ask him to let you have his ladder for me. I just want to borrow it till tomorrow, to clean the top shelves of my larder.'

'But I don't want to have to carry a ladder all the way back here!' said Lazy Luke in horror!

'All right. No ladder, no new-laid egg,' said Mother Cranky, and shut the door in his face.

'I'll fetch the ladder, I'll fetch it!' shouted Lazy Luke. 'You get the egg!' And away he went again, grumbling loudly.

'Fetching and carrying like this! What do people think I am? An errand-boy?'

He came to Father Hoo-Ha's little house and knocked at the door. But Father Hoo-Ha wasn't indoors, he was right at the bottom of his garden. So Lazy Luke had to go round the back way and walk all the way down to him.

'And what's brought *you* so far from your fireside today?' said Father Hoo-Ha.

'Mother Cranky says, please will you lend her your ladder?' asked Lazy Luke.

'What! Do you mean to say you've offered to carry it to her?' said Father Hoo-Ha, astonished. 'Wonders will never cease. Well, it's in my shed, so I'll have to get it out. You go round to Mr Long-Whiskers while I'm getting

54

it, and ask him to lend me his bicycle, please. He always lends it to me when I want it.'

'Oh *no*,' said Lazy Luke. 'No, I can't do that! I can't ride a bicycle and I'm not going to walk all the way back here pushing one!'

'Well, then – no ladder,' said Father Hoo-Ha, turning back to his gardening. 'No bicycle, no ladder – see?'

Lazy Luke did see. He sighed. 'I'll get the bicycle – but all I hope is that Mr Long-Whiskers hasn't got a job *he* wants doing as well. I'm tired of doing jobs.'

'Tired? You're always tired, you are, Lazy Luke!' said Father Hoo-Ha. 'It's a wonder to me you ever get up in the morning, it really is. Well now, do go along, or I shall have the ladder ready for you before you're back!'

Lazy Luke went off, groaning. His legs felt shaky and his head ached. Oh how tired he felt, doing so many things for so many people!

Mr Long-Whiskers was baking cakes, and he wasn't very pleased to see Lazy Luke. 'What do you want?' he said. 'You're just in time to do a job for me. Look, my oven isn't hot enough. Will you just pop out to the wood behind my house and bring back some wood for it?'

'No, I won't,' said Lazy Luke. 'Good gracious, that's what *I* wanted for my own fire, and here I've come for miles and done all kinds of jobs so that I can borrow some from Dame Hurry-About! If I'd wanted to fetch wood I'd have done it for myself, not for you!'

Mr Long-Whiskers picked up a broom and gave Lazy Luke a hard spank with it. 'You do as you're told!' he said. 'You haven't told me yet why you've come.'

'Oh – to borrow your bicycle for Father Hoo-Ha,' said Lazy Luke. 'Please don't spank me again with that broom. I'll go and get the wood for you!'

And away he hurried to the wood, gathered a great armful of dead wood, and hurried back. He did hope that Mr Long-Whiskers had put that broom away!

He had – and he had got the bicycle out ready for Lazy Luke. 'Oh, thanks,' said Lazy Luke and wheeled it off at once. But he was so tired that he really felt as if he must ride it. So he tried – and fell off at once. Goodness, what a crash! He bumped his head very badly indeed, and after that he decided to wheel the bicycle. He came to Father Hoo-Ha's and asked him for the ladder.

'Here's the bicycle,' he said. 'Oh my goodness – what an enormous ladder! Haven't you a smaller one?'

'No,' said Father Hoo-Ha. 'Ha – perhaps it will do your lazy bones good, carrying that all the way to Mother Cranky!'

Poor Lazy Luke. He staggered along to Mother Cranky's with the enormous ladder, and let it drop in her garden with a sigh of relief. He knocked at the kitchen door.

'I've brought the ladder,' he said. 'Can I have the egg?'

'Egg? What egg?' said Mother Cranky. 'Bless us all, what do you mean?'

'You said you'd give me a new-laid egg for Mr Borrow-A-Lot if I fetched that ladder,' said Lazy Luke. 'You did, you did!'

'Dear me, yes – I remember,' said Mother

Cranky. 'You've been so long that I'd forgotten about it. Here it is.' Lazy Luke took it
and went off to Mr Borrow-A-Lot. Goodness,
how far he had walked! He looked at his shoes
– just see, one of his toes was poking through
his shoe! Now he would have to pay for it to be
mended!

He came to Mr Borrow-A-Lot's house and
looked in at the window. Well, he was still
having cups of tea out of Dame Hurry-About's
teapot! Would you believe it! Lazy Luke was so
cross that he walked straight in at the door
without knocking.

'Manners, manners!' said Mr Borrow-A-
Lot. 'You want the teapot, I suppose? You've
been so long that I've brewed another pot.
Have a cup?'

'*No*,' said Lazy Luke angrily, and put the
new-laid egg down on the table. 'You ought to
have had it washed and ready for me.'

'You can go and wash it yourself if you talk
like that,' said Mr Borrow-A-Lot. 'And by the
way – could you lend me ten pence? I don't
seem to have any money left.'

'Ho! Haven't you! How strange – neither
have I, Mr Borrow-A-Lot!' said Lazy Luke.
He took the teapot and rinsed it angrily under
the tap. Really, the things he had done this
afternoon! He would have made a fortune if
everyone had paid him for his work! He took

the teapot to Dame Hurry-About's, and, oh dear, what was this? There was a note on the door for Lazy Luke. This is what it said: 'To Lazy Luke. I got tired of waiting for you. Leave my teapot on the doorstep. You can come for the wood tomorrow morning at ten o'clock. Dame Hurry-About.'

'Well! WELL! So all those jobs had been done for nothing – he couldn't wait till tomorrow to have wood for his fire. He would freeze to death in his little cottage. Lazy Luke put the teapot down and began to sniffle.

'Why didn't I get my own wood? Now I've got to go and find some, and I'm so tired and cold. I've walked so far. I've fallen off a bicycle and bumped my head. I've done lots of silly jobs. All because I was too lazy to fetch my own wood! Oooh-hoo-hoo!' And off he went to the woods, crying tears down the front of his suit. Poor Lazy Luke. We could give you some good advice – but what's the use? You'd never take it!

7

The magic rubber

Once upon a time Snooty the gnome found a most remarkable rubber. It lay on the ground, in the middle of the woodland path, a large, long rubber, pointed at one end, and round at the other.

'What a curious thing!' said Snooty, picking it up. 'It must be magic. I wonder what it does.'

He rubbed it idly against a young birch tree – and to his immense surprise the tree vanished!

'I've rubbed it out!' said Snooty, in amazement. 'Oooh! What a very magic rubber this is! It rubs things out!'

He went to a blackberry bush and rubbed the leaves with the rubber. They disappeared at once. Then Snooty rubbed a few toadstools with the strange rubber. They vanished too! How very astonishing!

'Hoo!' said Snooty, in delight. 'This rubber will be very useful to me. I can think of a whole lot of things I'd like to rub out!'

Snooty put the rubber carefully into his

pocket. Then he danced home, singing and whistling, for he was very pleased to think he had found such a wonderful thing.

He didn't tell anyone about the magic rubber. He meant to have a good time with it without anyone knowing! The first thing he did when he got home was to get out his best pair of shoes and rub a nail that was sticking up into the heel part. It always tore his sock – but now he could get rid of it!

Sure enough, the nail disappeared at once! The magic rubber rubbed it out! Snooty was pleased. He looked round to see what else he could rub out.

'Oh, yes,' said Snooty, 'I'll rub out the door between the kitchen and the hall. It's always swinging and banging, and I don't need it!'

So he rubbed the door out with his rubber! It was marvellous to see it go! It just went.

Then Snooty saw in his garden Whiskers, the black cat from old Dame Topknot next door. Now Snooty hated this cat because it sat on his flower-beds, and spat at him if he went near it. So he looked at it with a grin, and said, 'Ha! I'll rub you out, Whiskers!'

And out he went with the magic rubber – and do you know, he rubbed that black cat out! One minute Whiskers was there, and the next he wasn't! It was most extraordinary!

Snooty was delighted. What a fine rubber he

had found! He looked over the high wall and saw that Dame Topknot had a plum-tree full of ripe plums. If only he could get some! He knew Dame Topknot was out, for he had seen her go by with her shopping-basket.

'I can't climb this high wall – but I can rub it out!' he said. 'Good! I'll rub a neat hole in it, get through it, and take some of those plums before Dame Topknot gets back!'

So he rubbed part of the wall with the large rubber – and he rubbed so many bricks out that a big hole came. Snooty climbed through it and filled his pockets with plums! What a feast he would have!

Snooty had a good time with his magic rubber! He rubbed out a dog that came into his front garden. He rubbed out all the wasps that came sailing into his kitchen. He rubbed out a mess he made when he spilt a pail of dirty water over the floor! Dear me, the things he rubbed out!

And then Snooty did a very silly thing! The next day he heard a rat-tat at his door and he went to open it. Outside was Mister Biscuit the baker, with his bill. Snooty hadn't paid Mister Biscuit for a very long time, and he owed him a lot of money. Mister Biscuit had come to ask for it. He walked into Snooty's kitchen and put his bill on the table.

'Will you please pay me for the bread and

the cakes and the pies you have had?' he asked.

'I haven't any money at present,' said Snooty. 'I will pay you next week.'

'That is what you always say!' said Mister Biscuit angrily. 'I won't listen to you any longer!' And he banged his fist so hard on the wooden table that a teapot jumped off and fell to the ground – crash!

'You careless fellow, look what you've done!' shouted Snooty, in a rage.

'Pay me my bill and I'll give you two pounds to buy a new teapot!' said Mister Biscuit, his long beard bristling.

'Never!' said Snooty. 'Take yourself off, and take that dreadful beard with you!'

'It's a beautiful beard!' shouted Mister Biscuit.

'It ought to be cut off and made into a yard-broom for sweeping up rubbish!' cried Snooty rudely. And do you know what he did? He took out his rubber and rubbed out Mister Biscuit's beard! Mister Biscuit did look funny without it.

'What have you done?' he wept. 'Oh, my beautiful, beautiful beard! It took me forty years to grow it!'

'Well, grow it again,' said Snooty, 'and grow your hair again too!'

He rubbed Mister Biscuit's hair – and that

went as well! Mister Biscuit gave a squeal of fright and rushed out of Snooty's house. He ran down the street, weeping.

Everyone came out to see what was the matter, and when they heard how Snooty had rubbed out Mister Biscuit's beard and hair they were very angry.

'That is the magic rubber belonging to the Wizard Hurry-up,' they said. 'He will be very annoyed when he knows it has been used by Snooty. Let us go and tell him. No doubt that rubber has rubbed out Dame Topknot's cat, and made that hole in her wall, and rubbed out

Gobo's dog too. Dear, dear, to think that Snooty might rub us all out if he wanted to!'

The Wizard Hurry-up was angry when he heard that Snooty had found and used his rubber. He strode off at once to Snooty's cottage and banged so hard at the door that Snooty nearly jumped up to the ceiling with fright.

Snooty was too much afraid to open the door, but the wizard didn't wait – he just flung the door open and walked in.

'Where's my rubber?' he shouted to Snooty.

Snooty took it out of his pocket and gave it to Hurry-up without a word. Hurry-up took it and then rubbed it in three places on the ceiling and in four places on the walls. Big holes appeared!

'Other people can play about with a magic rubber too!' said Hurry-up. 'But I don't expect you'll be pleased when the rain and the wind come through these holes, Snooty. Next time you find something belonging to somebody else just think twice before you take it and use it in such bad ways!'

He went away, and Snooty stared dolefully at the big holes in his roof and walls. The wind blew through, and he shivered. Oh, dear! It would take him such a long time to mend those holes!

Snooty worked hard for a whole week mending the seven big holes – and then he saw, in his back garden, Whiskers, Dame Topknot's cat, sitting down on his flower-bed again. He stared and stared – for he knew that he had rubbed Whiskers out with his magic rubber.

And then he saw Gobo's dog in his front garden – and then he saw his kitchen-door swinging and banging just as it used to before he rubbed it out!

Snooty ran to the Wizard Hurry-up and told him what had happened. 'Everything has come back again,' he said. 'Did you know it would, Hurry-up?'

'Oh, yes,' said Hurry-up grinning. 'The magic lasts only a week – then whatever was rubbed out comes back again!'

'And would the bits of my roof and ceiling that you rubbed out have come back again too?' asked Snooty.

'Of course,' said Hurry-up.

'And here I've been working hard all week long trying to mend those holes!' groaned Snooty. 'What a waste of time and money – and how my poor back aches!'

'It serves you right!' said Hurry-up.

'You are very horrid,' said Snooty.

'If you talk to me like that I'll get my rubber and rub *you* out!' said Hurry-up. 'Now let me see, where did I put it – in this drawer, I think!'

But before Hurry-up could get his rubber,

Snooty was gone. You couldn't see him for dust! He wasn't going to be rubbed out, not he!

Mister Biscuit's hair and beard came back again, and he went marching off to Snooty's with his bill once more. And Snooty paid it without a word. And how he has behaved himself since that week! He's always afraid Hurry-up will be after him to rub him out, you see!

8

The little blue kitten

'What's that sitting on Dame Grumpy's window-sill across the road?' said Gobbo, looking out of his front door.

'Good gracious! It looks like a kitten – but it can't be, because it's as blue as the sky!' said his brother Winky.

'Let's go and see,' said Gobbo. So they ran across and leaned over the wall. 'Yes,' said Gobbo, 'it *is* a blue kitten. Well, I've never in my life seen a blue kitten before. Puss, Puss, Puss!'

Dame Grumpy looked out of the window at once. 'Now, just you leave my kitten alone!' she said. 'I know you two mischievous little goblins! If you dare to tease my blue kitten I'll rub spells on your noses and make them grow as long as cucumbers!'

'Oh no, please don't,' said Gobbo, in alarm. 'We're not mischievous, really we're not. You're thinking of our cousins Hoppy and Jumpy – they really *are* naughty. We only just came to look at your blue kitten. I suppose you wouldn't let us play with it sometimes? We could give it an empty cotton-reel to roll about – it would love that.'

'You leave my blue kitten alone!' said Dame Grumpy. 'If I see you anywhere near it I'll come after you with my Spanking Slipper!'

'Meow!' said the kitten, looking at Gobbo and Winky.

'There! It's talking to us!' said Gobbo, very pleased. But Dame Grumpy picked it up and went indoors with it at once.

'We'd better be careful,' said Gobbo. 'I don't like that Spanking Slipper of hers. Let's go back.'

Well, the two little goblins didn't go near the blue kitten. They just waved to it when they went out to do their shopping, but that was all. Then one day as they took their big round basket with them to shop at the market, they saw that the kitten wasn't on Dame Grumpy's window-sill as usual.

'It must be indoors,' said Gobbo – and just at that minute Dame Grumpy came out, calling 'Puss, Puss, Puss!' Then she saw the two goblins and frowned.

'Have you taken my kitten to play with? You know what I told you – I'll rub a spell on your noses and . . .'

'Please, Dame Grumpy, we haven't seen the

69

kitten this morning,' said Gobbo, in a hurry, backing away quickly. 'We've never even stroked it, though we'd like to!'

'Well, if I see you with it, I'll spank you, just as I said,' said Dame Grumpy. 'Puss, Puss, Puss, where have you gone to? Oh dear – I do hope it hasn't run away!'

'Come on, let's go and do our shopping,' said Gobbo. 'My goodness – I'd certainly run away from Dame Grumpy if I was her kitten – wouldn't you, Winky?'

They went off down the road. They were soon at the market, and bought such a lot of things: six rosy apples; six big brown eggs; some butter; a round chocolate cake; and a string of nice fat sausages. The basket was quite full by the time they had finished. They set off home again – and then, just as they passed under a big chestnut tree, they heard a sound that made them both stop at once.

'Meow! Meeee-ow! Meeeeeee-ow!'

'That's a cat mewing – and it's frightened!' said Winky at once. 'Where is it? Puss, Puss, Puss!'

'Mee-ow-ee-ow-ee-ow!' said the cat, wherever it was.

'It sounds as if it's up this big tree,' said Gobbo, and he looked up into the branches. 'Yes – it is! And, Winky – it's the little blue kitten!'

'So it is!' said Winky, peering up too. 'It must have wandered away from Dame Grumpy's and climbed up this tree. Perhaps a dog frightened it.'

'Come down, kitty!' called Gobbo. 'Come along. We'll take care of you. You needn't be frightened of dogs.'

'Meeeee-ow-ow!' said the kitten, sadly, and didn't move at all. It was much too frightened. The ground looked a long way away, and it was afraid of falling. It had never been up a tree before, and it didn't much like it now it was there.

'Little kittens shouldn't climb big trees,' said Gobbo, looking up at it. 'Winky, what can we do? We can't leave it there. It might never come down.'

'Well, I'll climb up and see if I can get it,' said Gobbo, and up he went. But as soon as he came near the kitten it climbed a little higher! But at last Gobbo managed to catch it and it snuggled into his arms.

'Oh good!' called Winky. 'Come on down.'

'I can't!' said Gobbo. 'I want my arms to climb down with, but I can't use them because I'm holding the kitten. I shall fall if I don't use my arms. Oh dear, don't wriggle so, kitten. Winky, what shall we do?'

'I don't know,' said Winky, and he frowned. Then a good idea came into his head. 'Gobbo!'

he called, 'shall I empty out all the things in our basket, and climb up the tree with it? We could put the kitten into it, and lower it down the tree.'

'But what shall we lower it with?' said Gobbo.

'I'll pop into Ding-Dong's house, and ask him if he'll lend me his kite-string,' said Winky. So he ran to Ding-Dong's house, and Ding-Dong said yes, certainly he could borrow his kite-string. So it wasn't long before Winky was back again. He emptied everything out of the basket, and tied the string to the handle. Then he climbed up the tree with the basket.

'Here we are!' he said to Gobbo. 'Now – put the kitten very carefully in the basket. I'll climb down, and you can let the basket swing down to the ground. I'll be there to take out the kitten.' Well, they were *just* doing that when Gobbo gave a yell that almost made Winky fall out of the tree.

'Winky, quick! Look, there's that wicked little Hoppy down there – and Jumpy too – and they're picking up all our shopping. Quick, climb down and stop them!' Winky climbed down so fast that he almost lost his footing! But when he came to the bottom of the tree, Hoppy and Jumpy had gone – and so had the brown eggs, the rosy apples, the butter, the nice fat sausages and the

round chocolate cake! Oh, those bad little goblins!

'Just wait till I see them!' said Winky, almost in tears. 'Gobbo, swing the basket down now, gently, very gently. Oooh – careful! I do hope the kitten won't jump out!'

The kitten lay quietly as the basket swung down – and even when Winky caught it, the little thing didn't move. It seemed to like the basket, it gave a little purr, shut its eyes and went to sleep!

'Dear little kitten!' said Winky. 'Oh dear – I'm glad to have rescued you, but you've made us lose all our shopping!'

Gobbo climbed down and the two goblins went off, carrying the sleeping kitten in the basket – and whom should they meet round the corner, but Dame Grumpy!

'Oh my goodness!' said Gobbo, and stopped. But it was too late – Dame Grumpy had seen the kitten in their basket.

'*You* had my kitten after all!' she cried. 'You took it away in your basket! I'll put a spell on your noses to make them long as cucumbers! I'll get my Spanking Slipper, I'll . . .' But the goblins didn't wait to hear any more. They fled down the road, and into their house with the kitten – and slammed and locked the door! When Dame Grumpy came panting up, they called from their bedroom window.

'You shan't have your kitten back till you promise not to put a spell on us. It was up a tree and we rescued it! We emptied our shopping-basket and borrowed Ding-Dong's kite-string, and let it down in the empty basket – and while we were doing that Hoppy and Jumpy stole all our shopping.'

'You get us back our shopping and you can have your kitten!' shouted Winky.

'Is this all true?' said Dame Grumpy. 'Well, I'm very, very sorry I chased you. I'll make a spell straight away to bring back your shopping!' And hey presto, she waved her stick in the air and muttered some strange magic words.

Good gracious! What was this flying through the air? A string of sausages! Six brown eggs, followed by six rosy apples! A pat of butter and a round chocolate cake! They all came quietly to rest on the garden seat. Gobbo and Winky could hardly believe their eyes.

'Now come on down with my blue kitten,' said Dame Grumpy. 'You're very kind. I'm sorry I was so cross – but it isn't often that goblins are helpful, you know.'

So Gobbo and Winky came down into the garden, carrying the sleeping kitten in the basket. It looked so sweet and comfortable. 'We'll lend you the basket till it wakes up,' said Winky. 'Please – do you think we could come and play with it sometimes?'

'Of course. Whenever you like!' said Dame Grumpy. 'But just let me warn you – keep indoors for the next ten minutes. I'm sending my Spanking Slipper after those two bad goblins, Happy and Jumpy!'

So Gobbo and Winky kept safely indoors – and goodness me, they saw that Spanking Slipper hopping along the road, looking for the goblins!

'There it goes, looking for Hoppy and Jumpy,' said Gobbo, with a giggle. 'My word – won't they get a shock when it hops into their kitchen!'

They will – but I don't feel a bit sorry for them, do you?

9

Oh, Flibberty-Gibberty!

Now once, on a lovely windy spring morning, little Flibberty-Gibberty felt full of glee. He leapt and he danced as he went through the primrose woods, and he shouted for joy. Then, just for fun, he pretended that something was after him. 'I must run, I must run!' he shouted at the top of his voice. 'The Big Blustery Breeze is after me! Ooooh!'

He leapt into the air as he ran, like a little mad thing. 'Ooooh! It's after me! The Big Blowing Blustery Breeze is after me! It'll blow me to the moon! It'll sweep me to the stars! Make way, make way. I'm running for my life. Ooooh!'

The rabbits leapt out of his way in fright. A robin trilled after him, 'Tirra-tatta, what's the matter?' But little Flibberty-Gibberty wouldn't stop.

A squirrel ran up a tree out of his way, and Flibberty-Gibberty raced by, his cloak blowing out like a sail. 'Ooooh! Get out of my way! I shall be caught by the Big Blowing Blustery Breeze.'

A little fawn jumped out of his way just in time, and stared after him with big startled eyes.

Why was Flibberty-Gibberty acting like this? Who was after him? The little fawn was frightened and raced after the pixie at top speed.

Then some rabbits ran after the fawn, afraid too. What was this Big Blowing Blustery Thing that Flibberty was shouting and leaping and dancing about?

The brownies smiled to see the mad little pixie go leaping. Whatever would he do next? One called after him.

'Flibberty-Gibberty, be careful of the Wandering Wizard. He's about this morning, and he's in a very bad temper. Don't you let him turn you into a toadstool and sit on you, as he did to Bron the Brownie!'

That made Flibberty-Gibberty slow down a little. The Wandering Wizard – oooh! He wasn't very nice. Nobody liked him much, but nobody could catch him, because he was much too clever.

But then Flibberty forgot about the wizard, and went flying through the woods as lightly as an autumn leaf, leaping and bounding as he went, still pretending to be scared to death!

And then, round a tree, who should he bump into and knock right over but the Wandering Wizard himself! My goodness me, what a thing to do! The Wizard went over like a wooden skittle and lay there, all his breath knocked out of him.

'Out of my way!' shouted Flibberty-Gibberty, not seeing who it was at first. 'The Big Blowing Blustery Breeze is after me – oooh!'

'What's that?' cried the Wandering Wizard, clutching Flibberty by the ankle. '*Who's* coming? What's happening? My goodness, look at this fawn coming at top speed – and all these rabbits. *What's happening, I say!*'

'Let go my ankle! Run, run!' shouted the little pixie. 'Run! I tell you the Big Blustering Blowing Breeze is coming! It'll blow you to the moon! It'll sweep you to the stars. Run!'

Just then the wind did blow, and very roughly too, so that the little clouds scudded across the sky like white rabbits. The Wizard felt quite scared. He still held Flibberty's ankle and wouldn't let go.

'Help me up!' he said. 'I don't know what to do. I'm too old to run away. Oh, this wind – *I* don't want to be blown to the moon! Flibberty-Gibberty, help me up, I say!'

'Well, let go my ankle then,' said Flibberty, quite fiercely. 'I must run. I tell you, the Big,

Blowing, Blustery Breeze is after me! Let me go!'

'You must help me first, before I let you go,' said the Wizard, and stood up very carefully. He held Flibberty's arm now, and still wouldn't let him go.

'Whoooooooooosh!' said the wind, entering into the fun. It blew the Wizard's hat off, and Flibberty picked it up for him. The little pixie was frightened. Oh dear – he didn't want to be taken away by this Wandering Wizard! *What* a pity he had bumped into him.

'Whooooooooosh!' said the wind again, and tried to pull off the Wizard's flapping cloak.

'Take your fingers off me, you Blustery Breeze!' shouted the Wizard in fright. 'Flibberty, what can I do? I'll be blown right away, for my big cloak will act like a sail!'

'Climb up into a tree!' shouted Flibberty, longing to get rid of the Wizard. 'I'll help you.'

So he helped him up into a tree – and then the wind rushed down again in delight and shook the tree so that it bent from side to side and swayed like a ship!

'I shall be blown out!' shouted the Wizard. 'And here comes the wind again! Flibberty, I shall be *blown out*, I tell you. Think of something!'

'Give me your girdle and I'll tie you safely to the tree!' cried the pixie. 'Ooooh – your hat might get blown to the moon. It will be waiting there for you, when *you* arrive if I don't tie you up. Give me your girdle!'

So the Wizard undid his girdle with one hand, clinging to the swaying tree with the other – and Flibberty tied him very, very tightly to the tree. Oh, very tightly indeed!

'You needn't be afraid of the Big, Blowing Blustery Breeze now!' shouted the pixie. 'If it blows all day and all night you'll be safe here,

Wizard. Whooosh, here comes the wind again. Goodbye, goodbye – it's blowing me away again!'

And off he went once more, leaping, bounding just like the little fawn behind him, pretending to be dreadfully frightened. 'Oooh! I shall be caught. Make way for me, I shall be caught!'

But he wasn't caught. Nor was the little fawn, nor were the skippitty rabbits or the scampering squirrel. Only one person was caught and that was the Wandering Wizard tied so tightly to the tree. How he howled for help, as loudly as the wind! How he shook with rage, so that the tree swayed even more!

'Flibberty, come back! Untie me! Get me down! Flibberty, I'll turn you into a candle-flame and blow you out! I'll turn you into a lump of ice and melt you. I'll – I'll . . .'

But Flibberty-Gibberty was far away, tired out with all his leaping and jumping and pretending, fast asleep with the tired rabbits and squirrel and little fawn cuddled up to him. What a day! What a wonderful, blustery, windy day!

'It was fun,' said Flibberty in his dreams. 'Oh, it was FUN!'

10

Tippitty and the dolls' house

'What shall I do today?' said Ellen. 'I'm tired of all my toys, and I've read all my books!'

'Well then – what about giving your dolls' house a spring-clean?' said Mummy. 'I had a look at it yesterday and really it is too dirty and untidy for words!'

'Oh yes – I could do that!' said Ellen. 'Can I have a saucer of water, and a little cloth, Mummy?'

'Yes – and you can have this tiny little nail-brush to brush the carpets and scrub the floors,' said Mummy. 'It's such a nice dolls' house, and I'm sure the little dolls who live in it must feel very uncomfortable – everything is in such a muddle!'

Well, Ellen soon had a saucer of warm water with some soap powder in it. She had two little cloths, one for the windows and one for floors. Mummy gave her a tiny duster too, to polish the furniture.

It was certainly a pretty dolls' house from the

outside. It had white walls, a red roof, four chimneys, windows that opened – and a tiny garage at the side.

The whole front opened when Ellen wanted to play with the dolls' house. Even the lights switched on and off, and water came out of the taps from a small tank in the roof. Ellen could even fill the bath when she liked!

She began to spring-clean the house. She took down the curtains first. Then she took out the carpets and rugs. Then out came all the furniture, and soon the house was empty.

And then Ellen noticed a strange thing. The little dolls' house dolls weren't there!

'Where are they?' wondered Ellen. 'There should be four of them, all tiny little things. I haven't seen them for a long time – but then I haven't played with my dolls' house for ages.'

The toys who sat around watching Ellen could have told her what had happened to the tiny dolls! The teddy bear had been a great friend of theirs, and they had told him how they hated living in such a dirty, untidy little house.

'We'd clean it ourselves,' they said, 'but we haven't any cloths or brooms or dusters. We can hardly see out of the windows, they are so dirty!'

'Well, there's a lovely dolls' house in the toy-shop just down the road,' the teddy bear told them. 'There aren't any dolls in that. Why don't you slip out one night, and let me take you to the shop? Then you could live in that nice new dolls' house, and be sold with it, when somebody buys it!'

'That's a good idea,' said the oldest doll, a pretty little thing in a blue silk frock. 'We'll go tonight.'

And so that night the bear had opened the front door of the dolls' house and called in softly. 'Are you awake? I'm ready to take you!'

The dolls were awake. They all trooped out of the front door, and the oldest doll shut it quietly. 'I'm not a bit sorry to leave!' she said. 'Ellen never even comes near us, and hasn't played with us for weeks! Lead the way, Teddy, to our new home.'

And off they all went, out of the door, down the stairs, and through the kitchen door, which had been left open for the cat to come in. They soon arrived at the toy-shop, and the teddy bear lifted each tiny doll up to the letter-box on the front door, and slid her through it. It was lucky that the letter-box was so low down!

'Thank you!' the dolls called softly. 'We can see the lovely dolls' house. It will be fine to live in a clean house. Perhaps a nice little girl will buy it one day and we'll all go and live with *her*!'

So that was why Ellen's dolls' house had no

dolls living in it now! She simply couldn't *imagine* where they had gone to! She hunted for them everywhere, and the toys watched her, nudging one another.

'Wish we could tell her!' said the teddy bear. 'She would feel sorry she hadn't kept the dolls' house nice and clean then!'

'Sh!' said the big doll. 'She'll hear you! Now look – she's beginning to scrub the floors – about time too!'

It took Ellen the whole day to clean the dolls' house. She washed the curtains and Mummy ironed them. She cleaned the floors and the windows. She rubbed down the walls. She brushed each little carpet and each rug, and washed three that were very dirty indeed. Then she polished all the furniture – the little tables and chairs and cupboards, and the wardrobe that stood in the bedroom. She even polished the tiny bathroom taps, and put a very small towel on the rail there.

She filled the little tank in the roof with water, so that the taps would run properly.

'Now the bath can be filled too,' she said. 'But there isn't anyone to have a bath in it! Oh dear – *where* can my dolls have gone!'

Mummy was very pleased when she saw the spotless little house. 'Now your dolls will really *like* that,' she said. 'Where are they?'

'I don't know,' said Ellen. 'They've

disappeared. Do *you* know where they are, Mummy?'

'No, I don't,' said Mummy. 'They'll be here somewhere, I expect. I'll have a look round.'

But neither she nor Ellen could find the dolls. 'You'll have to save up and buy one or two,' said Mummy. 'It's a pity that that dear little house shouldn't have anyone living in it!'

The toys thought so too. The big doll went to look through the windows, and said how lovely it looked inside. The bear peeped in too, and wished he was small enough to sleep in one of the little beds. 'They look so cosy,' he said. 'I do wish we knew someone who would like this little house.'

Then the teddy bear remembered the pixie who lived in a hole in the apple tree, just outside the playroom window. He turned to the big doll in excitement.

'What about Tippitty the pixie?' he said. 'She's always saying how cold she is at night, even though she has stuffed the hole in the tree with dead leaves. Do you think *she* would like to live in the dolls' house now that it is so lovely and clean? She's just the right size!'

'Oh *yes*!' said the bear, who liked Tippitty very much. 'We'll ask her this very night.'

So they tapped seven times on the window-pane, which was a signal for Tippitty to come and see them. She flew in at the top of the window, and landed just beside them.

'What do you want?' she said. 'Oooh – I had to get out of my leafy bed – and it's *such* a cold night!'

'Come and see the dolls' house,' said the bear. 'It's clean and lovely now!'

Tippitty pressed her nose to one of the dolls' house windows and looked inside. The moon was shining brightly, and she could see everything clearly. It certainly did look very pretty and very cosy. 'I'd like to go in at the front door,' she said. 'Oh, what a pity – whoever cleaned the house forgot to clean the little brass knocker!'

She went in at the front door and explored the whole house, while the big toys watched her through the windows. She could hardly believe it when water came out of a tap she turned on – and she loved the little mirror on the dressing table. 'I've never had a mirror in my life!' she said. 'Oh – I *do* wish I could live here!'

'Well, you can,' said the big doll at once. 'The dolls who once lived here have run away to the toy-shop, so the house is empty. You come, Tippitty. We'd love you to!'

'But – suppose Ellen peeps inside!' said Tippitty. 'She might see me and catch me. I couldn't bear that!'

'You could easily hide in the big wardrobe in the bedroom,' said the bear. 'Oh do come, Tippitty. It would be fun to have you to play with each night. I'll keep the tank filled, so that you can have a bath whenever you want to. And when Ellen is out we could light a fire in the kitchen for you!'

'All right. I'd love to come,' said Tippitty. 'This very night! Shall I be able to sleep in this dear little bed – and wash myself in that little basin? I shall keep this house very, very clean and tidy if I live here!'

Well, she did go to live there and she is there still! She sleeps in the little bed, she has a bath when she wants to, and, when Ellen is out, the bear lights the little kitchen fire, and Tippitty sometimes bakes tiny fruit cakes for him!

And HOW tidy and clean she keeps the house! Ellen's mother is always so pleased when she looks in at the window to see it.

'Well, really, Ellen keeps her dolls' house beautifully now!' she says. 'What a pity no one lives in it. I do wonder where those little dolls went to!'

Ellen herself is very puzzled. One morning she looked in at the bedroom window of the dolls' house and saw that the little bed wasn't made!

And then she noticed that the tiny brass knocker on the front door was bright and shining!

'Good gracious! Surely nobody is *living* here!' she thought. 'Is one of my dolls back – or is it a small mouse who likes a cosy bed? I must look into every little room and see.'

So she looked in the kitchen and the sitting-room and the bathroom and the bedroom, and even the garage. But she didn't see anyone at all.

90

Tippitty was hiding in the wardrobe, of course, shivering with fright. Oh, dear – would Ellen find her there and turn her out?

But Ellen didn't once think of looking in the wardrobe. So Tippitty is still living in the dolls' house, but now she is careful to make her bed as soon as she jumps out of it.

You'll know where to look for her if ever you go to tea with Ellen! Inside the wardrobe!

11

The little green imp

The Prince of Ho-Ho had a very bad-tempered cook. None of the other servants liked her, but she was big and strong, and nobody dared to complain of her.

They had a very bad time until Twinkle, the kitchen-boy, came to work there. Mrs Pudding, the cook, made him get up at five o'clock in the morning, and would not let him go to bed until midnight, and the poor boy was working hard all the time.

But Twinkle had a grandmother who was half a witch, and when he got out one afternoon to run an errand he went to his grandmother's cottage in the wood.

'Granny!' he said, 'tell me what to do! There's a cook at the castle, and she gives me a dreadful time, and everyone else too! How can I stop her?'

His granny thought for a moment, and then she nodded her head. 'Wait a minute!' she said. 'I've just the thing for you!'

She took a big green dish and filled it full of water. She scattered a green powder into it and it changed the water to a brilliant emerald. She peeled a potato into it, stirred it round with a peacock's feather, and muttered words so magic that Twinkle felt a bit frightened.

'Watch!' said his granny. He looked into the bowl, and suddenly out of the green water there jumped a green imp with a potato body and a grinning face! He smacked his hands together and looked up at Twinkle's grandmother.

'You'll do!' said the old lady, and she laughed. 'Here, Twinkle, put him into your pocket. As soon as you get into the kitchen, put him on a shelf and leave him. He will do the rest!'

Twinkle thanked his grandmother and put the green imp into his pocket. The imp laughed out loud and pinched him once or twice, but Twinkle didn't mind. He guessed that the imp would play a few tricks on Mrs Pudding, the bad-tempered cook!

As soon as he got into the kitchen he put the imp on the shelf behind a saucepan. Mrs Pudding turned round and scolded Twinkle. 'What have you been so long for, you good-for-nothing boy?'

'Now, Cookie, you be good!' said the voice of the green imp suddenly from the shelf. 'Naughty, naughty, naughty!'

Mrs Pudding turned round in a rage, too astonished to speak. The green imp peeped at her from behind a saucepan and made a face.

'And what are *you* doing in my kitchen, I'd like to know!' said Mrs Pudding, her eyes gleaming with rage. 'Come here!'

But that little imp stayed where he was, rapping out a tune on one of the saucepans, and grinning with all his might. 'Oh, Cookie, what a naughty temper!' he shouted.

The other servants were all staring in delight and astonishment. How could that green imp dare to speak to Mrs Pudding like that? The cook went over to the shelf and put out her hand to get the imp, but he picked up a fork lying nearby and rapped her fingers hard. Then he pushed six saucepans on to the floor, one after another – bang! – crash! – smash! – bang! – crash! – smash! – what a dreadful noise they made! Mrs Pudding was very angry.

She picked up a newspaper and folded it so that she might hit the little imp with it. She brought it down on the shelf – bang! Two more saucepans and a kettle jumped off to the ground – bang! – crash! – clang! The imp was nowhere to be seen.

'That's finished *him*!' said Mrs Pudding, pleased. But, dear me, it hadn't! No, he had just jumped neatly off the shelf on to the kitchen table behind the cook. And on the

table he saw a jug of milk. The imp grinned. He picked it up by the handle, jumped up on to the mantelpiece, and tilted the jug over Mrs Pudding's head!

Trickle, trickle, trickle! The milk fell on her head and ran down her neck! She got such a shock! How that imp laughed! He nearly fell off the mantelpiece with laughing. As for Twinkle and the other servants, they roared too. But Mrs Pudding got angrier and angrier.

She picked up a large cabbage and flung it at the imp. He dodged it neatly and it hit the

95

kitchen clock. Crash! Down came the clock and a big tea-caddy, and the cabbage too! The cook stared in horror!

'Oh, naughty, naughty, naughty!' said the imp, dancing about on the table again, where he had jumped.

Mrs Pudding turned round to him, and the wicked little thing threw an egg at her. It broke and went down her neck to join the milk. Oh dear – poor Mrs Pudding! What a sight she looked! The imp began to laugh so much that he was afraid he might be caught, so he jumped up on to another shelf and hid in a bucket there. Mrs Pudding looked all round for him, and when she could not find him she went to wash the egg off herself.

'How dare you all stand grinning there?' she cried to the other servants. 'Get on with your work at once, and if you see that green imp anywhere about just catch him and bring him to me!'

But nobody meant to catch him. It was fun to see someone who was not afraid of Mrs Pudding! She washed herself and then boxed Twinkle's ears for upsetting some salt.

'Oh, naughty Cookie, oh, naughty Cookie!' squealed the voice of the green imp, and he popped his head out of the bucket. Mrs Pudding saw him.

'Oh, so you've turned up again, have you?'

she said. 'Well, I'll get you this time!' And with
that she took the bucket down from the shelf,
but the imp hopped out and ran into the larder
crying, 'Can't catch *me*, can't catch *me*!'

Mrs Pudding rushed after him, but he was
waiting for her. He threw a string of sausages
round her neck and dropped a pat of butter
neatly on her head from the top shelf. Really,
you never knew what that wicked imp was
going to do next!

All the evening things went on like that, and
there was no catching that imp, and no stopping him either. Twice he emptied water over
Mrs Pudding, and once he pelted her with
apples he had found in a basket. Mrs Pudding
rushed round and round the kitchen after him,
but she couldn't seem to get hold of him at all.
He was as slippery as an eel. He undid her
shoe-laces when she wasn't looking. He undid
her apron-strings and made her apron slip off a
dozen times. He emptied pepper near her, and
she sneezed thirty times without stopping.

'Oh, won't someone get rid of this horrid
little imp for me!' wept Mrs Pudding at last.
'What has he come for?'

'I think he has come to tease you and tor-
ment you because you have treated *us* so
badly,' said Twinkle boldly.

'That's right, that's right, that's right!'
squealed the imp from somewhere under

the table, where he was busy untying Mrs Pudding's shoe-laces again.

'If only you'd catch him and get rid of him for me I'd mend my ways and be better,' sobbed Mrs Pudding, who was quite tired out.

'Very well, then, I'll try,' said Twinkle, grinning to himself. He knew just what to do, for his granny had told him. He took a pat of butter, a dab of vinegar and a brown clove. He stuck the clove into the butter and smeared it with vinegar. Then he held it out to the imp.

The little green imp smelt the clove in the butter and came eagerly for it. Twinkle snatched him up and put him into his pocket.

'I'll go and give him to my old Granny,' he said to Mrs Pudding. 'She will know what to do with him, for she is half a witch.'

He ran off, chuckling to himself, and soon came to his grandmother's. When she heard his story, how she laughed! 'That will cure her bad temper!' she said. 'Tell Mrs Pudding that I will take the imp, but I shall not be able to keep him if she loses her temper again, for he will surely come back!'

So Twinkle left the green imp with his granny, who set him to work polishing her kettles and saucepans till they shone. He was afraid to do anything cheeky to the old dame. She had made him from a potato, and she could turn him back into one again!

As for Mrs Pudding, she didn't dare to lose her temper again, for she was so afraid the imp would turn up in her kitchen once more. So now everything is peace and quiet there, and Twinkle the kitchen-boy is as happy as can be.

But he can't help wishing Mrs Pudding would lose her temper once or twice – it *would* be such fun to see that imp dodging about the kitchen shouting, 'Naughty Cookie! Naughty, naughty!' at the top of his cheeky little voice. I'd rather like to see him myself, wouldn't you?

12

Winkle makes a mistake

Winkle was a mean and dishonest old gnome. If he found a bad coin he pretended it was a good one and gave it to a shopkeeper on a dark evening. If he could borrow anything and not return it, he did. His house was quite full of basins, brooms and plates he had borrowed and never taken back!

'You'll be sorry one day!' said the people who knew him. 'Yes you will! People like you don't get on well in this world!'

But Winkle only grinned – for he really got on very well indeed. He had a long red stocking put away full of money. He always had chicken every Saturday for dinner, which his black cat caught for him from the farm over the hill, and he always had warm clothes to wear in winter.

'I get on all right!' he said to himself. 'What's the sense of being honest if it keeps you poor? No, no – I'll go my own way and be rich!'

So he went on being mean and dishonest, and getting richer and richer.

Now one day he went shopping in the next town. He bought all kinds of things, and asked the shops to send them home to him. The only parcel he took home was a brown paper one with his mended shoes inside.

He caught the bus and sat down. Next to him was a very smart fellow, a gnome who lived in a big castle in the next village to Winkle. He took no notice of Winkle at all, although the gnome said 'Good morning.' He didn't like the look of Winkle, it was plain.

Winkle got out at his village, picked up the brown-paper parcel and walked home, feeling very cross with the fine gnome who hadn't said 'Good morning' to him. He put down his parcel and put on the kettle to boil.

After he had had a cup of cocoa and some bread and cheese he opened his parcel to take out his mended old shoes – and what a surprise he got!

In the parcel was a pair of very fine shoes indeed – oh, very fine ones, fit for a king to wear! They were of leather sewn with gold, and had gold laces threaded through, and buckles set with pearls. Winkle stared at them in astonishment.

'The old cobbler at the shop has put the wrong shoes in my parcel!' he thought to himself. 'Silly old fellow! How careless of him! Well, I'm not going to bother to give them back to him. He shouldn't have been so silly as to make that mistake! I shall keep them and wear them! Ho, ho!'

Wasn't he mean? He ought to have taken them back at once to the cobbler, of course. He put them away in his cupboard and longed for a party so that he might wear them and be very grand indeed.

Now it wasn't the cobbler who had made the mistake at all. He had put the right shoes in the gnome's parcel – Winkle's old mended ones. It was *Winkle* who had made a mistake – for in the bus he had sat next to the smart gnome who had also a parcel with him; and in *his* parcel was a pair of very fine shoes he had been to buy for His Majesty the King! Winkle hadn't looked to see that he was taking the right parcel when he jumped from the bus – he had picked up the parcel belonging to the other gnome and gone off with that.

So when the grand gnome arrived home and opened *his* parcel, what should he find but a pair of old mended shoes and he was most disgusted. He guessed at once what had happened. The other gnome in the bus, the one who had said 'Good morning' to him, must have taken the wrong parcel. Oh, well, it was annoying, but no doubt when the other fellow found out his mistake he would bring back the shoes.

But, of course, Winkle didn't. As you know, he put them into his cupboard and kept them for himself, thinking that the cobbler had made a mistake.

Now when the grand gnome didn't get the shoes brought back, and found that nobody had asked the bus-conductor about them, he decided to put up notices everywhere, to say what had happened, and to tell the gnome who had taken the wrong parcel where to bring the shoes. So he wrote some notices in red ink and stuck them up all over the place, in the villages round.

At the top of the notice he printed three words very large indeed. The words were: 'GOLD-LACED SHOES'. Anyone catching sight of those words and having the wrong shoes at home would be sure to read the notice, thought the grand gnome, and he would soon have the shoes back.

Well, it wasn't long before Winkle the gnome did see those notices, and read the words at the top: 'GOLD-LACED SHOES'. But he didn't read any further.

'It's only that silly old cobbler putting up notices about the shoes he gave me in mistake for my own,' thought Winkle. 'Well, if I don't read the notice, I can't find out anything more about the grand shoes, and as I don't *want* to find out anything, I shan't read the notice!'

So he didn't – and he was the only person in the village who didn't know that the shoes belonged to the King himself!

Well, when no one brought back the shoes to the grand gnome in his castle he became angry.

'Someone is keeping them for himself!' he thought. 'Oho! Well, I can soon stop that! Shoes, come to me, and clatter as you come!'

Then a most extraordinary thing happened. Those gold-laced shoes, put safely away in Winkle's cupboard, began to struggle to get out. They wriggled out of the door and began to make a clatter on the floor. Winkle heard them and ran to see what was the matter.

When he saw that the shoes were trying to get away he was surprised and angry and put them back into the cupboard again.

But once more they struggled out, almost breaking the door down! They wriggled away from Winkle's hands and danced downstairs. They shot out of the front door with Winkle after them and clattered off down the street, making a great noise.

'Stop! Come back!' yelled Winkle, who wasn't going to lose those fine shoes if he could help it. But the shoes took no notice at all. They just went on, making a great clatter all the way down the street. Then people poured out of their houses to see the strange sight, and followed Winkle and the shoes, laughing and pointing. What an excitement for the village! Wherever were those shoes going?

The shoes went clattering to the next village and climbed up the steps of the castle where the grand gnome lived. He heard them coming and went to meet them. He saw behind them an angry gnome, trying in vain to catch hold of the dancing shoes.

'Take this man,' the big gnome ordered his servants. 'Bring him before me in my castle.'

He picked up the shoes, and strode inside, the servants following with the surprised Winkle between them. Winkle was truly amazed. Why was he suddenly treated like this?

He stood before the grand gnome.

'How came you to have these shoes?' asked the gnome sternly.

'Oh – the c-c-cobbler put them into my parcel by m-m-mistake,' stammered Winkle, in fright.

'Why didn't you take them back to him, then?' said the gnome.

'Well, if he was silly enough to make a mistake I thought he should be punished for it,' said Winkle, more boldly.

'I see,' said the gnome. 'You think if people make mistakes they deserve to be punished, even if they didn't mean to make them?'

'Certainly,' said Winkle.

'Well, listen to a little tale I have to tell of a gnome who made a big mistake,' said the grand gnome, in a stern voice. 'Once there were two gnomes in a bus, each with a brown-paper parcel. One gnome had old mended shoes in his parcel, but the other had gold-laced shoes he had bought for His Majesty the King. Now one of the gnomes got out of the bus first and by mistake took the wrong parcel.'

Winkle grew pale. How dreadful! So it wasn't the cobbler's mistake after all – it was *he*, Winkle, who had made a mistake!

'As you have just said,' went on the grand gnome, 'a mistake must be punished, even though it was not made on purpose! You will go to prison, or pay a fine of one thousand pounds to the poor people of the villages around! Oh, Winkle, you think I have not heard of you and your mean, dishonest ways – but your name is in everyone's mouth! You are rich – but only by wrong-doing! Now you shall be poor, and also by wrong-doing! Well – which is it to be – prison – or one thousand pounds?'

'I haven't got one thousand pounds,' wailed Winkle. 'I've only seven hundred in my long red stocking at home.'

'Bring me that,' said the gnome. 'And work hard and honestly for the rest, which you must bring to me as you earn it. And remember this, Winkle – riches got by ill means will sooner or later fly away, even as yours have done! Now go!'

Winkle stumbled home, sobbing and crying, to fetch his hoard of money. He was bitterly ashamed of himself. His neighbours pointed at him and nodded their heads.

'We told him so!' they whispered to one another. 'Meanness and dishonesty only come to one end!'

Poor Winkle! He is working hard every day now. His hoard of money is gone, and he is trying to earn more to make up the thousand pounds. But he has learnt his lesson. If he borrows, he pays back. If he finds what isn't his, he gives it back to the owner at once. He doesn't cheat, he doesn't shirk. And it may be that by the time he has earned enough money to pay the thousand pounds, he will be a different person – straight, honest and true.

I hope so, don't you?

13

What a surprise!

Barry was very fond of birds, and every morning he put out crumbs for them, and a saucer of fresh water. He made a bird-table, too – just a piece of wood on the top of a pole – and from it he hung strings of unshelled peanuts which he had carefully threaded together, and a coconut with a hole made at each end. He put all kinds of titbits on the table, and you should have seen the birds that came to visit it!

When Barry's birthday came, the postman knocked at the door and left three parcels, a small one and two big ones. Inside the small one was a silver pencil – and inside the two big ones were wooden nesting-boxes to put up in the garden for the birds to nest in! Barry was so pleased.

'Just what I've always wanted!' he said, looking at the two boxes in delight. They were very nicely made, and the top part, which made a slanting roof, could be lifted up – so that Barry would be able to peep inside and see if any bird had begun to nest there.

'I shall put these nesting-boxes up this very day,' said the little boy. 'I shall put one in the chestnut tree – I know a fine place there – and one I shall fasten among the rose-ramblers. There is such a small hole in each for the birds to get in and out that I am sure only the tiny tits will make their homes there. What fun it will be!'

So out he went very happily into the garden, and soon the two nesting-boxes were in their places. One was well hidden among the ramblers and the other was neatly hung on the trunk of a small chestnut tree, protected by an overhanging branch.

'If I were you, Barry,' said his mother, 'I would hang up bits of fat or peanuts near your new nesting boxes, and then, when the tits come to them, they will see the boxes, and perhaps think they are good nesting-places.'

So Barry hung up a few peanuts by each box, and a piece of suet too. In ten minutes' time the tits had found the nuts and the suet, and were very busily pecking away at them. Barry could hear them calling to one another in excitement.

'This is suet, this is, this is suet, this is! Peanuts, peanuts, peanuts! This is suet!'

The tits were pleased to find more food in the garden. They thought that Barry was the nicest, kindest boy in the world, and they were always happy in his garden. One of them flew to the top of a nesting-box. He wondered what it was – it hadn't been there before. He hopped about all over it, sometimes the right way up, sometimes upside down. He didn't really mind whether he swung one way or another!

Then he called to his wife, 'Come and see!'

She flew down to him. 'Look!' said the tit in excitement. 'There is a little hole here. It leads into a nice dark room. Let us go inside and see whether it would be a good place to nest in.'

So in they went, and they both decided that it would be exactly right. This was the box that Barry had put in the rose-ramblers. The other box was taken by another pair of excited tits, who were most delighted to find such a fine nesting-place.

'It's near plenty of food!' they sang. 'It's in the garden of the nicest boy in the world! There are no cats! We shall be safe, safe, safe!'

Then they began to build their cosy nests. They made them of the softest things they could find – bits of moss taken from the ditch, a great many hairs from the post against which the brown horses in the field rubbed themselves each day! And some hairs from the dog next door. When he shook himself a few hairs flew from his coat, and the tits were always on the watch for these. They would hunt about the lawn for them.

Then they lined their nests with soft feathers. Some they found in the hen-yard, and how they squabbled with the sparrows over them! The sparrows liked the feathers too, to make a lining for their nests, and tried their best to take them all – but the tits pounced down in a trice, and carried off most of the downy feathers under the very beaks of the angry sparrows!

The nest of the tits in the rose-rambler box was finished first. It was so cosy and warm. Barry knew that they were building there, for he watched them carrying moss and hair in their beaks to the ramblers. He was delighted. One day, when he knew that both the tits had left the nest, he went quietly to it and lifted up the roof-lid. He gazed inside before he shut down the lid, and to his great delight saw five pretty little eggs. Now there would be crowds of fluffy yellow baby tits calling all over the garden to their parents!

He ran indoors to tell his mother.

'I'm so glad,' she said. 'But if I were you, Barry, I wouldn't peep inside any more. The tits may not like it, and it would be so dreadful if you made them desert their nest and leave their eggs or young ones. It does sometimes happen, you know.'

So Barry did not go and peep for a long while. When he did the next time he got a great surprise, as you will hear.

Now, as you probably know, all birds and animals can see the little folk, although very few of us humans can do so. The tits especially are friendly with them, for the fairies love the merry, pretty little birds, with their bright voices and amusing ways.

Very often the tits went to the woods nearby where many elves lived, and in their hunt for small insects they came across many of the little folk and talked to them. And one day the tits that nested in the rose-rambler box found an elf of great use to them.

She lived in a hole at the foot of an old oak tree. The two tits often went to hunt for insects in the bark and the elf liked their merry voices, and always popped her little golden head out to wish them good day.

One morning the tits were hunting in the oak tree bark when a gun went off not far away. It was the farmer shooting rabbits. It frightened the tits so much that they rose straight up into the air to fly – and one of them flew full-tilt into the branch overhead and hurt himself so badly. that he fell down to the ground in a faint, his eyes closed, and his wings drooping.

'What's the matter, what's the matter?' called his little wife, in a fright. She flew down to her mate, but he did not move. Then she heard a scampering of feet not far off and saw the bright-eyed weasel, whom all small creatures and birds fear, for he feasts on them.

'Help! Help!' cried the little tit, in a panic, and she flew up into the air. The weasel stopped – and then came running over to the oak tree.

But before he could snap up the poor little tit someone came rushing out of the roots of the oak. It was the golden-headed elf. She caught up the tiny tit and ran back with him into her home. He was safe there, for the weasel could not possibly squeeze into the small hole where she lived.

'I'll pay you out for that!' he shouted at her and ran off, mad with rage, for he was hungry.

In a few minutes the tit opened his eyes and stretched his wings, none the worse for his bump. When he found the elf bending over him, and heard what had happened, he was very grateful indeed.

'It is most kind of you!' he said, in his shrill little voice. 'Most kind indeed! Let me know, elf, if you want help yourself at any time, and my wife and I will be very pleased to do whatever we can for you!'

Then off he flew with his wife, back to his nest in the box, where he rested all day and was soon quite himself again. When their eggs hatched out into five pretty little youngsters, the two tits were mad with delight. They sang about them until everyone in the garden was quite tired of hearing how beautiful and how marvellous the baby tits were. But indeed they really *were* very sweet, for they were just bundles of blue and yellow fluff.

One day the robin brought a message to the two tits.

'Blue-tits!' he sang, 'I bring a message to you from the elf in the woods. She is very unhappy and bids you go to her.'

Off went the tits at once. The elf was not in her usual place under the oak tree – but they found her shivering in the ditch not far away, with only a cobweb shawl wrapped round her.

'What is wrong?' cried the tits, flying down beside her.

'Oh, little friends,' said the elf, 'a dreadful thing has happened to me. The weasel was so angry because I saved the life of one of you the other day that he vowed to force me to go away. He sent an army of red ants into my cosy home and they ate up all my pretty clothes, and bit me so hard that I could not stay there any more. Now they are building their nest in the oak tree roots, so I have no home. I don't know where to go, because if I choose another hole the ants will come after me there too. Now, here I am, cold and hungry in this ditch, with only this cobweb shawl to keep me warm. I am so dreadfully afraid that the weasel will come after me.'

'You poor little thing!' cried the tits, cuddling close to her. 'What can we do for you? Let us think hard!'

So they thought very hard, and then the little hen tit cried out in delight.

'I know! I know! Let the elf come to live with us in our nesting-box! It is true that we are rather crowded now that we have five babies – but it is warm and cosy, and the elf will have

116

plenty of company and be quite safe from the weasel there!'

'Oh, that would be wonderful!' said the elf, tears of joy coming into her eyes. 'Oh, there is nothing in the world that I would like better! I could look after the babies for you when you went out together, couldn't I!'

'Yes, you could!' cried both tits, delighted. 'There is one of our children who is far too bold. We are afraid he will climb out of the little entrance hole one day and fall to the ground. Then the weasel will be sure to get him. If *you* were living in the nest with us we should never be afraid of leaving the babies alone. Do come!'

The elf spread her pretty, gleaming wings, and flew up into the air with the tits. The weasel, who was hiding in the bushes not far off, gave a snicker of rage. He had been hoping to pounce on the elf that very day.

The tits took the elf to their nesting-box. She was just too big to squeeze in through the little hole, so she had to lift up the roof and get in that way. She cuddled down among the fluffy babies and was soon as warm as toast.

How happy she was there! And how pleased all the seven tits were to have her! She was so good to them all. She looked after the five babies carefully when the two parents were away, and wouldn't let the bold one try to climb out of the hole. She saw that each baby had his share of the food in turn, and would not let the strong ones rob the weak ones. She brushed their feathers and told them tales. They loved her very much indeed.

She was very warm and cosy there, and had plenty to eat, for the little tits brought her all kinds of food each day. They knew which flowers had the sweetest honey, and they were very clever at bringing leaves with dewdrops on them, so that the elf could drink. Nobody knew that the elf lived in the box, not even the other tits. It was a secret.

And then somebody found out. Guess who it was! Yes, it was Barry. He did so badly want to see how many baby birds the tits had in the rose-rambler box. So one sunny morning he tiptoed to it, after he had seen the two big tits fly out, and he lifted up the roof-lid to see inside.

He looked down – and there, looking up at him were five fluffy yellow baby-tits – and one pretty, golden-headed elf! She was cuddled down among the tits, her arms round them, the prettiest sight you could imagine!

Barry was so surprised that he simply stood and stared. Then he quietly shut down the lid and went away. It was the greatest and loveliest surprise of his life – a real secret that he couldn't tell anyone at all.

When the big tits came back, the elf told them what had happened. She was frightened. 'I must fly off!' she said. 'That boy will come back and take me away.'

'No, no,' sang the tits at once. 'Don't be afraid of Barry. He is the nicest boy in the world! He would not harm us, and he will not harm you. You are quite safe here. Let him peep at you if he wants to. He will never, never hurt you!'

When the five baby tits flew away into the garden in the bright summer-time, the elf stayed in the nesting-box and made it her home. She tidied it up, and she made a small cupboard for herself and a shelf where she put all her belongings.

'Do come back and nest here next year,' she begged the tits, who often came and peeped in at the hole to talk to her.

'We will!' they promised. 'We certainly will!'

So there the elf still lives, as Barry knows very well! He peeps at her once a week, and she knows him well now and smiles gaily at him. He has never told anyone his great secret – but I know because the tits told the robin and he sang it all to me! And how I'd love to go and peep in that box – wouldn't you?

RUN-ABOUT'S HOLIDAY
and other stories

Illustrated by Joyce Smith and David Dowland

Contents

IT all began on the day when Robin and Betty left their little wooden engine and its trucks out on the lawn.

They had hurried in to their dinner—and had forgotten all about the red engine and its coloured wooden trucks. They didn't go out to play afterwards because it began to rain.

Suddenly Robin remembered the little train and went to the window. "Betty—we left the wooden train out on the grass!" he said. "It will get wet and the paint will be spoilt. I'll go and bring it in."

"I'll come with you," said Betty. "Let's put on our macks and sou'-westers—it's nice to go out in the rain!"

So out they went, down the garden to the lawn where they had been playing. "We left the train here," said Robin, looking all round. "Where's it gone?"

It wasn't there. "We *did* leave it here, didn't we?" said Robin, puzzled. Then he suddenly caught sight of a bit of bright red under a bush. "Oh, there it is," he said, and went to the bush.

He pushed aside the leaves—and gave a
cry of surprise. "Oh—here it is—and I say
—there's somebody in it! Hey, little fellow,
who are you?"

The two children gazed down at their
engine with its coloured trucks. In the cab
of the engine was a small man with a very
long beard, pointed ears and bright green
eyes. His coat was as green as the leaves
around.

The little fellow looked up at them in surprise and then leapt off the engine. He dived
under the bush—but Robin dived after him!
Betty gave a loud squeal.

"Oh, what is it—who is it—what's he
doing here?"

Robin came out of the bush, his face red
with excitement. In his hand he held the
little green-coated man, who was wriggling
and shouting.

"Put me down! Let me go! I wasn't
doing any harm!"

Robin stood him gently on a garden-seat,
still holding him. The rain had stopped,
and the sun suddenly came out, so that all
the garden was a-sparkle with rain-drops
hanging on the leaves. There seemed to be
magic in the air!

"Who are you?" asked Robin. "And what are you doing with our engine?"

"I didn't know it was yours," said the little fellow, his eyes shining very green. "I'm Run-About the brownie, and I live in Brownie-Town."

"Why, goodness me—isn't that Fairyland?" said Betty, excited.

"Well, it's *part* of Fairyland," said Run-About. "The nicest part, we brownies think. Now, do please let me go."

"Not yet," said Robin. "What were you doing with our engine?"

"Well, you see, I'm a messenger—that's why I'm called Run-About," said the brownie, "and I was told to take a message to the squirrel who lives in your garden. It's a long way here and I was tired—and when I saw your lovely engine lying here all alone, I thought I could use it to take me back to Brownie-Town."

"But it doesn't go by itself, silly!" said Betty, laughing.

"I know. But I can make it go all right," said Run-About. "I always carry quite a lot of magic with me."

Betty and Robin felt so excited that they hardly knew what to do next! Why, this little man might have come straight out of their story-books! Were they dreaming? No—two people couldn't have the same dream. It was real.

"Let's take him into our playroom," said Robin. "I'd like to ask him a lot of questions!"

"Yes, let's," said Betty. "We'll leave the engine here now it's stopped raining, and fetch it afterwards. Come on, Robin—bring little Run-About."

"You will let me go, won't you?" said Run-About, as they went indoors, Robin carrying the little brownie gently in his hand.

"Yes, we will. But it *is* so exciting to meet someone like you," said Robin. "We can't let you go just yet! You come and see all our toys!"

They were soon in the playroom, and then Robin put the small man down on the floor. Door and windows were shut, so he couldn't run away!

Run-About gazed round in surprise. "Oh, what a lovely place! Oh, look at that little house—why it would just be big enough for me!"

"It's my dolls' house," said Betty. "You

"It would just be big enough for me!"

can open the front door and go inside, if you like!"

But the little man had now caught sight of Robin's clockwork car, and he ran over to it in excitement. "A little car! Just my size, too!"

He was so pleased and excited about everything in the playroom that Robin couldn't help laughing.

"Oh, what a lovely tea-set!" said Run-About, when he saw Betty's dolls' tea-set. "And oh—*look* at this magnificent aeroplane —and here's a boat! What a lovely place this is! Can I come and visit it whenever I like?"

"Yes," said Robin, pleased. "But Run-About—can we visit you too? Please say yes!"

"Of course!" said Run-About. "I'll take you to my home straightaway—if you'll let me drive that wooden engine of yours!"

"Come on, then!" said Robin, in excitement. "Let's go out into the garden again and find the engine. Quick, Betty, come along. Oh, what an adventure this will be!"

ROBIN, Betty and Run-About the brownie ran out into the garden. The brownie ran as quickly as a little mouse. They came to the wooden engine and trucks, lying where they had left them.

The rain had quite stopped now, and the sun was hot. "I'm too warm in my mack and sou'-wester," said Robin. "Put them in the shed, Betty."

Betty ran with them to the shed. The small brownie got into the cab of the engine, smiling all over his face.

"How can *we* get in?" asked Robin. "We're too big."

"Easy!" called back the brownie. "I'll make you small! Put your foot into one of the trucks—you too, Betty—and shut your eyes. Quick, now!"

Each of the children put their toe into a truck, and shut their eyes. A big wind suddenly blew—and they gasped, their breath taken away. They opened their eyes.

Goodness me, what had happened in that moment? "We've gone small!" cried Robin.

"We're small enough to get into a truck!
How did you do it, brownie?"

"I felt just as if I was going right down in
a lift!" said Betty, sounding out of breath.
"You did some real magic then, didn't you,
Run-About?"

"Yes. I told you I always carried some

"It's a butterfly," said Run-About cheerfully

about with me," said the brownie. He
hopped out of the engine and bent down to
its wheels. Robin looked out of his truck to
see what he was doing.

"I'm rubbing a bit of Get-Along Magic

into the wheels," said Run-About. "That's all this engine wants to make it go!"

He climbed back into the cab and beamed round at the children. The engine had two trucks, and Robin was in the first one, Betty in the second.

"All ready?" he asked. "How does it feel to be small like me?"

"Nice," said Betty. "But oh dear, the bushes seem ENORMOUS and those daisies over there look so big that I could sit quite comfortably on their yellow middles! Ooooh —what's that?"

"It's a butterfly," said Run-About, cheerfully. "A peacock butterfly, that's all! Looking for honey, I expect."

"It's as big as an eagle to us!" said Robin, as the pretty thing flew over them. "Let's go, Run-About. I do want to find out how you get into Fairyland from here!"

"Well, there are entrances in all kinds of places," said Run-About. "Sometimes a hollow tree leads to Fairyland, sometimes a rabbit-hole, sometimes a cave in a hillside. But not many people know these. I know most of them, of course."

The wooden engine suddenly began to creak and groan. "We're off!" said Run-

About, pleased. "The magic is working in the wheels. Hold tight!"

The wooden wheels of the engine suddenly began to turn and off went the little train, making a rattling noise.

It ran out from under the bush, over the grass, and on to the path that went to the bottom of the garden.

"Oh—there's Gardener!" said Robin. "Quick, he mustn't see us!"

But it was too late. The engine and trucks rattled past his legs, and he gave a yell of surprise.

"Hey—what's this!"

Robin and Betty laughed and laughed as they rattled past him. They went right down the path to the hedge at the foot of the garden, and through a gap there into the field beyond.

"Hold tight now," said Run-About, "we're going down a rabbit-hole, and we'll be in the dark for a bit. Hold tight!"

They held on tightly to the sides of the trucks as the engine shot down a big rabbit-hole. Well, well—to think that one of the entrances to Fairyland was so very near their own garden! Who would have thought it!

It was quite dark in the rabbit-hole, and

the children could see nothing at all. Suddenly they stopped at a wide place in the burrow, and saw two gleaming eyes looking at them. Then something soft brushed past them, and they went on once more.

"That was a rabbit," explained Run-About. "We waited at a passing-place so that he could get by. I expect you saw his eyes."

"Yes, I did. I wondered what they were, they looked so enormous!" said Robin. "Run-About, is everyone in Fairyland as small as you?"

"Pretty well—except for a giant or two," said Run-About. "But you needn't worry about them—we only keep good ones in Fairyland! Ah—here we are—the other end of the tunnel!"

The engine ran out into daylight, and the sun suddenly shone down again on Robin and Betty. They gazed round in delight. Everything seemed the right size now. Trees grew here and there, and fields lay around, gleaming with flowers that the children didn't know.

Then Robin saw a peculiar tree—it really and truly looked as if it had biscuits growing on it instead of flowers!

"Stop, Run-About," he said. "I want to look at that tree. It makes me feel hungry!"

"Oh, that?" said Run-About. "Yes, it's a biscuit tree. Do hop out and pick a pocketful—they're most delicious!"

Dear me—*what* a lovely land to come to!

IT was very exciting to pick biscuits off a tree. Robin and Betty picked quite a lot and then went back to the train. Robin nibbled one.

"Oh—it's *lovely*!" he said. "It tastes of honey."

"Of course," said Run-About. "It's a Honey Biscuit tree. And over there is a Chocolate Biscuit Tree, look. And we'll soon be passing a Sausage Roll Bush—most useful if you happen to be late for dinner. But we mustn't stop any more."

The engine started off again, rattling along well, keeping to paths or roads, and pulling its two trucks easily.

Run-About was very proud to be driving it. All the people they met stared in wonder at him, and he felt very important indeed.

The children sat in the trucks and munched the delicious honey biscuits, looking at everything they passed. They went through a most exciting market, where little folk of all kinds bought and sold.

"A fairy with wings, look!" said Betty

"And more brownies like Run-About. And that must be a wizard. Robin—see his pointed hat and flying cloak!"

Pixies, elves, brownies, imps, gnomes— all the many folk of Fairyland were there. And the buildings were as interesting as the people!

"Look at that tower reaching right up into the clouds!" said Robin. "And surely that glittering place over there must be a palace?"

"Yes. It belongs to Prince Bong," said Run-About. "It has fifty thousand windows, that's why it glitters. And that's the castle belonging to Wizard Hoo-Ha over there. Once it disappeared when a spell he was making went wrong—we were all *so* surprised. But it came back the next day."

"This must be a very, very exciting place to live in," said Betty. "Oh, look at those dear little crooked cottages!"

"Do you like them?" said Run-About. "Mine is just the same. We'll soon be in Brownie-Town and I'll show you my own dear little cottage."

They ran into a small town with curious little shops and houses. Run-About stopped at the very end. The children looked at the cottage there.

"Oh—it's *lovely*!" said Betty. "Such funny chimneys! And a thatched roof. But there's no door, Run-About!"

"No. I have two doors, really, but when I go off on one of my journeys, I make a spell to turn them into part of the wall," said Run-About. "Then nobody can get in. I keep losing my keys, you see, but now I don't mind about keys—I just use a spell."

He jumped out, and took a pencil from his pocket. He drew a rather crooked outline of a door in the front wall, and a knocker on it. He knocked loudly—and hey presto,

"I don't mind about keys—I just use a spell"

his pencilled door became a real one—just as crooked as he had drawn it!

The children went inside. What a dear little place! Run-About went to a cupboard and opened it. Inside, on the shelves, were pies and cakes and tarts and biscuits—all kinds of delicious-looking things!

"Choose what you like and we'll sit down and have a talk," said Run-About. So soon they were sitting in funny little chairs, eating and talking as fast as they could.

"I told you I was a messenger," said Run-About, eating a big jam tart. "When anything goes wrong in Fairyland, a message is sent to me, and I have to go off to try and put it right. I mean—suppose a bridge breaks down, the message comes to me—and off I go to find someone to mend the bridge. I'm always running about all over the place—that's how I get my name, as I told you."

"Have you been very busy lately?" asked Robin, taking a bun full of cream.

"Very," said the brownie. "Too busy. I've been told to take a holiday. If I get too tired I can't do any magic, you see—then I'm not much use in Fairyland."

"Run-About—come and stay with *us* for

a holiday!" cried Betty, suddenly. "Do, please do! You can live in our playroom, with all our toys. You'd love that. And we'd play with you whenever we can. It would be a fine holiday for you!"

"Well—that's quite an idea!" said Run-About, his green eyes shining. "I think I will! But I'd have to leave my address with somebody in case I was wanted. Something might happen that only I could put right."

"Well, leave *our* address," said Robin. "Haven't you got anyone who would come with a letter to you, if things went wrong?"

"Yes. Plenty of creatures would help," said Run-About. "Mice or birds or even rabbits could be sent with a message. Yes— I'd love to come for a holiday with you!"

And that is how it came about that Run-About went to have a holiday with Robin and Betty, and how they came to share in many strange adventures. I really must tell you all about them.

Now—there they go, back to the playroom in the children's house, rattling along in the wooden train—but this time Robin is in the cab with Run-About, and Betty is in the first truck, waiting for *her* turn to get into the cab. You don't know what exciting things are going to happen, Robin and Betty. What fun you're going to have!

4 *A MESSAGE FOR RUN-ABOUT*

IT was very exciting to have a brownie living in the playroom! Nobody but Robin and Betty knew he was there, of course. He was very happy indeed, and lived in the dolls' house most of the time.

"The biggest bed just fits me," he said. "And I do love cooking on the little kitchen stove. Do you mind if I clean the house properly? It's rather dirty and dusty, and the curtains could do with a wash."

"Oh *yes*—please do," said Betty. "It's so difficult for me to clean all the little things there with my big hands! You *are* kind, Run-About. I do so love to see you popping in and out of the front door, and waving to us from the windows!"

Run-About played with all the toys, of course, and longed and longed to sail in the boat. So one night Robin smuggled him into the bathroom when he was having his bath, and Run-About bobbed up and down in the boat very happily.

"Make bigger waves!" he said. "Bigger ones still! That's right—it's just like the real sea!"

He told the children all kinds of curious tales—stories of witches and wizards, and spells and enchantments. He really was a most interesting visitor to have!

"I *am* enjoying this holiday!" he said. "Especially as nobody has been to bother me about anything. Thank goodness nothing seems to have gone wrong in Fairyland lately!"

It was funny he should say that, because that very afternoon a message came for him. It was brought by the robin. He came flying down to the window-sill with a piece of paper in his beak.

"It's for me," said Run-About. "Bother! I hope I haven't to go back home." He took the paper from the robin and read it.

"Oh dear—yes, something must be done about this. The little arched bridge over the stream near Brownie-Town has broken —and it *must* be mended before midnight because Prince Bong is coming back to his castle tomorrow—he's been away visiting his brother Bing."

"But—how can you possibly mend a bridge before midnight?" said Robin. "It would take our workmen *weeks* to do!"

"I'll have to think," said Run-About, and

he went into the dolls' house and sat down
on the little stool there, thinking hard.

He jumped up at last and came running
out of the little front door. "I've got it! I
can easily mend the bridge if you'll lend me
your Meccano set—you know, that collection
of bits and pieces that you build things with.
You made a lovely crane the other day."

"Oh yes—of course we'll lend it to you,"
said Robin. "On one condition! That we
come and see you mend the bridge!"

"Right!" said Run-About, beaming.
"Come on—we'll go in the engine. Take it
into the garden, and bring the box of Meccano things. Don't let anyone see us!"

It wasn't long before they were all speed-
ing away in the wooden train again! Robin
and Betty were as small as before, and very
excited. The Meccano box was in the last
truck.

Down the garden, through the gap in the
hedge and down the rabbit-hole! Rattle-
rattle, rumble-rumble—that wooden train
could certainly go fast when it had Get-
Along magic in its wheels! It ran out of the
rabbit-hole at last and there they all were
in Fairyland again. How lovely!

" We'll go to Brownie-Town and find the

broken bridge," said Run-About. "No—
we can't stop at that biscuit tree—sorry!
We'll do our work first and play and eat
afterwards!"

Too dangerous to travel over it

They came to the little stream and followed
the road beside it. But when they came to
the bridge that went over it to the other side,
they could get no farther—the bridge was

quite broken! It had sagged in the middle, and now it was too dangerous for anything to travel over it.

Two brownies were there, very pleased to see Run-About. "You're our only hope!" they said. "You and your good ideas! We've only got till midnight to mend this bridge, Run-About."

"Whatever happened?" said the brownie.

"One of the giants came along and stupidly walked over the bridge," said a brownie. "Crash! That was the end of it—and will you believe it, the giant grumbled because his foot had gone into the water and had got wet!"

"Those giants!" said Run-About, crossly. "Well it's QUITE impossible to mend the bridge, I'm afraid—but I've a much better idea."

"What?" asked the two brownies.

"These children have lent me a wonderful box of bits and pieces," said Run-About, and he showed them the box of Meccano. "It would be easier to build a fine new bridge than to mend the old one."

"What a fine idea!" said the brownies, and soon all the things were being emptied out of the big box. They seemed enormous to the children now, because they themselves were so small!

"Now!" said Run-About, rolling up his sleeves. "To work, everyone! We've *got* to build a bridge as fast as ever we can!"

IT was great fun trying to build a Meccano bridge over the little river. Robin took charge, because he had so often built all kinds of things in the playroom—cranes and bridges, signals, towers and goodness knows what!

The brownies were very sharp, and did exactly what Robin told them. Betty just handed the pieces one to the other, because she wasn't really very good at building and fixing things together.

"It's a good thing the pieces are so light," she said. "I hope they'll be strong enough for a bridge!"

"Oh yes!" said Run-About. "Anyway I can always add a Hold-Up spell if we're not sure. Does this piece fasten here, Robin?"

"Yes, that's right. I say, we *are* getting on," said Robin, pleased. "Shall we make half this side, and then go to the other side and make the other half there—and fit the middles together afterwards?"

"Good idea!" said Run-About. So they made half the bridge one side of the river, and then Run-About borrowed a tiny boat and they all rowed off to the other side.

Betty's job was to row backwards and forwards fetching the pieces they wanted. She worked very hard indeed!

Soon the other half of the bridge was built, and the two halves met in the middle! Robin very carefully joined them together— and the bridge was finished! It really was a fine one.

The children and the brownies looked at it proudly. "Couldn't be better," said Run-About, running to and fro over it. "As strong as you like! It doesn't even need a Hold-Up spell!"

"I wish we could see Prince Bong's carriage coming across to-night!" said Betty.

"Well—we'll see," said Run-About. He turned to the other two brownies. "Send a message to Prince Bong that a new bridge has been built for him. I'm going on holiday again!"

Off the three of them went in the little wooden train—and this time they stopped at the Chocolate Biscuit Tree and also at a tree they hadn't seen before, which grew jam tarts just like big open flowers!

"I wish we grew trees like this in our

They stopped at the Chocolate Biscuit Tree

world," said Betty. "Why don't we!"

They were all very tired that evening, and the children went to sleep quickly, wondering whether Run-About would wake them to see Prince Bong going over the bridge they had built for him!

But Run-About was fast asleep too, and it really looked as if nobody would wake up at all!

And then a tapping came at the playroom window—tap-tap-tap—tap! Tap-tap-tap!

Run-About awoke at once, ran out of the dolls' house and went to the window.

"Run-About? I've a message for you,"

said a small high voice, and a tiny pixie looked in. "The Princess Goldie was flying home from a dance to-night on her bat, and he stupidly got caught in the topmost branches of a tree—in your world here, too! She sent a message for you to go and help. Whatever can you do?"

"Goodness! *I* don't know!" said Run-About, astonished. "Wait—I'll go and wake two children here and see if they have any good ideas."

Then Robin suddenly felt his shoulder tapped and woke up with a jump to hear Run-About's voice by his ear. The little fellow was up on his pillow.

"Robin! A messenger has come to me. The Princess Goldie is in trouble. Listen!"

He told the boy all about it, and Robin got out of bed to wake Betty. Soon the three of them were having a little meeting.

"How can we get to the top of a big tree in the darkness, and rescue the Princess and take her home?" said Run-About. "This is the biggest puzzle I've ever had!"

"Run-About—I suppose you couldn't make our toy aeroplane fly, could you?" said Betty, suddenly.

"Of course! The very thing!" cried Run-

About. "I've often wanted to fly in that lovely little aeroplane. I've got plenty of Fly-High magic. I'll go and get it. You get the aeroplane!"

Well, it wasn't long before Robin, Betty, the pixie at the window, and Run-About were all in the aeroplane, the children made as small as the others! They were on the window-sill by the open window, ready to take off.

Run-About had rubbed a Fly-High spell on the wings of the plane, and they were beginning to make a curious humming noise. They quivered and shook—and then, with a swoop, the aeroplane was off into the night-sky, flying beautifully.

"Oh, how wonderful!" cried Betty, looking down at the moonlit world beneath her. "Oh, what a fine feeling it is to fly high like this!"

"Guide us to the tree where the Princess Goldie waits with her bat," said Run-About to the pixie. "We'll soon be there!"

How that toy aeroplane flew—really, it was the most exciting thing that had ever happened to the two children!

IT was quite a long way to the big tree, but at last the aeroplane arrived there. It circled over the very top, and Run-About looked down in the bright moonlight.

A small voice called out. "Oh, What's this? An aeroplane! Who is in it, please?"

"Me, Your Highness—Run-About the Brownie," called Run-About. "I got your message. I'll get the aeroplane to hover like a butterfly just over your branch—and if you stand up, we'll pull you in. Ready?"

The aeroplane hovered just over the bough where the Princess stood, and she stretched out her arms. Run-About and Robin pulled her gently up and into the aeroplane!

She was the prettiest little thing Robin and Betty had ever seen. "Like one of the pictures in our fairytale books!" whispered Robin to Betty.

"It's very kind of you to fetch me like this," said the Princess. "I really didn't know *what* to do! My bat hurt his wing when he flew into the tree—a most extraordinary thing for a bat to do, but I think he must have been very sleepy. I've bound up his wing and it will be better to-morrow. He's crept under a bough and hung himself upside down to sleep."

"We'll soon take you back to your castle, dear Princess," said Run-About. Robin gave him a nudge and whispered to him.

"Do we pass anywhere near the Meccano bridge we built?" he said. "I do so want to see Prince Bong going over it with his carriage!"

"Ah, yes," said Run-About, remembering. He turned to the princess. "Your High-

Up and into the aeroplane!

ness," he said, "would you like to see a
marvellous new bridge I and some friends
built to-day? I can easily hover over it."

"Yes. I would!" said the Princess Goldie.
"Somebody told me about it. It sounds
grand!"

"Look—what's that down there?" suddenly said Betty, looking over the side of
the aeroplane.

"It's Prince Bong's carriage on the road
home!" said Run-About. "Good! We'll
follow him and watch him use our bridge!"

So, in great excitement they flew above the
galloping horses and the shining carriage in
which they saw Prince Bong. "I can see the
river—we're coming to it!" cried Betty.
"Oh Robin—suppose our bridge wasn't
strong enough and broke just when Prince
Bong drove over it. Whatever should we
do?"

Everyone began to feel rather worried.
The carriage was drawn by eight horses,
and looked rather solid and heavy. Surely
the little light bridge they had made would
not hold the carriage and horses when they
drove right across. Why, oh why, hadn't
Run-About put a Hold-Up spell on the
pieces?

The horses galloped towards the bridge. The coachman slowed down a little as he came near.

"It's just a bit narrow," said Robin, watching. "Ah—there goes the first pair of horses on the new bridge!"

The first pair was followed by the second, and soon all the horses, and the carriage too, were on the bridge. Everyone in the aeroplane held their breath. What a load was on that little bridge!

But the bridge held! It creaked just a little when the carriage rolled on, but it held! It really was very well made, and Robin couldn't help feeling proud.

"It's one thing to build a *toy* bridge," he said to Betty, "but this one is a *real* bridge, meant to be used. Run-About, are you pleased?"

Run-About's green eyes shone brightly, and he nodded his head.

"Rather!" he said. "Well, we've been very busy to-day and to-night, haven't we? Making a bridge, and rescuing Princess Goldie! We'd better get on now, and fly to her castle."

Off went the aeroplane again, its little propeller whirring madly. Robin leaned

back in his seat. Who would have thought
that he would ever ride in his own toy aeroplane? It was really too good to be true!

"There's my castle," said Princess Goldie,
pointing over the side of the aeroplane.
Everyone looked down to see it.

It rose up high on a hill, quite a small
castle, but a beautiful one, with towers
soaring high. "It's got a draw-bridge!"
said Robin. "I've always longed to have a
draw-bridge let down for me!"

"Well, you shall," said the Princess. "I
want you to come in and have supper with
me. I haven't had much to eat at the dance
and I'm hungry."

So, to Robin's great delight, when the
aeroplane flew down beside the great moat
that circled the castle, the draw-bridge was
let down for him to walk over.

"You go first," said the Princess, "and
feel as grand as you like, Robin!"

So Robin walked over the draw-bridge,
feeling really very important indeed, and
the others followed. Then, with a creak and
a groan the draw-bridge was drawn up again
into place. Now no one could go in or out!

What a wonderful supper they had—and
dear me, what did Robin and Betty do after-

wards but fall fast asleep! Run-About laughed to see them.

"We'll never get them into the aeroplane again to-night!" he said. "They must sleep here."

But what would their mother say when she went into their bedroom next morning and found them missing? What a to-do there would be! Wake up, Robin, wake up, Betty, but no, they won't even open their eyes!

WHEN Robin and Betty woke up
next day they remembered all that
had happened the night before.
They had walked over the draw-bridge into
Princess Goldie's castle, they had had a
wonderful supper with her—and then they
had fallen asleep!

"We must be in the castle still—how
exciting!" said Robin, and he opened his
eyes.

But they weren't in the castle! They were
in their beds at home. Robin sat up in surprise. "But we *can't* be at home—we didn't
get back into the aeroplane, I know!"

He ran into the playroom to see if the toy
aeroplane was back. No, it wasn't. And
Run-About wasn't there either! How
strange. Then how did he and Betty get
back?

He went to talk to Betty and she couldn't
understand it either. They had their breakfast and then went back to the playroom,
feeling very puzzled.

Suddenly a whirring noise came to their ears—and in at the window flew the little toy aeroplane, shining in the sun! It landed on the floor very neatly and out jumped Run-About, grinning all over his little bearded face.

"Hallo!" he said. "I'm back again. I stayed the night in the castle and flew home after breakfast."

The children stared at him in surprise. "Well, then—how did *we* get back here?" asked Betty. "We didn't come in the aeroplane!"

"No. The Princess Goldie knew a very clever spell," said Run-About. "She rubbed a spell on your eyes to make you wake up in your own beds—and you did."

"But—but I still don't understand how we got here," said Robin, puzzled.

"Magic never *can* be understood," said Run-About. "So don't worry about it. Didn't we have an exciting time last night? I'm getting quite famous in Fairyland now, what with making bridges and flying aeroplanes!"

"Oh—then perhaps *another* message will be sent to you soon, to put something else right," said Betty, pleased. "I must say you're an exciting visitor to have, Run-About!"

"I wonder what your next message will be," said Robin.

He didn't have very long to wonder. When they were out in the garden after tea, playing hide-and-seek, a little red squirrel sat up in a tree, watching. Robin saw him and pointed him out to Betty and Run-About.

"Why—he's come to give me some news, I'm sure!" said Run-About. "It's Frisky, from Brownie-Town!" He beckoned to the squirrel, who bounded down at once.

The squirrel whispered into Run-About's ear. "Dear, dear," said Run-About, looking all round. "Where is he? Tell him he can come out of his hiding place, these children are my friends."

Then, to the children's surprise, from out of a clump of snapdragons came a funny little fellow, his hat in his hand. He bowed low to Run-About.

"Sir," he said, "I have heard of your fame, and how you built that wonderful bridge. People say you can do anything! So I have come to ask your help."

The children gazed at this funny little

man, no bigger than Run-About. He was dressed in very gay clothes, and his hat had an enormously long feather in it.

"A witch complained of the noise"

"Who are you?" asked Run-About, looking pleased.

"I am Mr. Heyho, the Roundabout Man, from the great Fair in Pixie Village," said the little man. "A dreadful thing has happened, sir."

"What is it?" asked Run-About.

"A witch complained of the noise that my roundabout music made," said Mr. Heyho, "and when I told her that I couldn't stop my roundabout just to please her, she was very angry. She flew over it on her broomstick and dropped a spell into the machinery that makes it work. . ."

"And now I suppose it won't go round and round any more!" said Run-About.

"You're right," said Mr. Heyho. "And I'm losing a lot of money, Mr. Run-About, and the owner of the Fair, Mr. Stamp-Around, says I'll have to take my roundabout away and he'll get another."

"Ah—I know old Stamp-Around," said Run-About. "A very hot-tempered fellow. Well, what do you expect me to do, Heyho?"

"I don't know, sir," said Heyho. "The witch's spell won't wear off for three days, I'm afraid. I thought perhaps you'd go and ask her to remove it."

"Good gracious! I wouldn't go near a witch for anything!" said Run-About. "I'm afraid I can't help you, Heyho."

"Couldn't you even find me a new roundabout for three days?" said Heyho, dolefully.

Run-About shook his head. "You can't buy roundabouts easily!" he said. "No— I'm sorry, but this time I can't do anything to help!"

Heyho turned to go, looking very sad. But before he had disappeared, Betty called out to him.

"Wait! Wait a minute! I've thought of something that might do. Something in the playroom."

"What do you mean? *We* haven't a roundabout," said Robin.

"Come up to the playroom and I'll show you something I think will do!" said Betty. And there they all go at top speed. Whatever in the world has Betty thought of?

SOON Robin and Betty were in the playroom with Run-About and little Mr.
Heyho. Robin was puzzled. What *had*
Betty got in her mind? He knew quite well
that there was nothing at all like a roundabout among their toys.

Betty went to the cupboard and rum-
maged at the back. She brought out a great
big humming-top! She put it down with its
pointed end to the floor, and began to work
the handle up and down that spun it.

Soon the great top was spinning all over
the playroom floor, humming as loudly as
a hundred bees! Heyho stared at it in the
greatest delight.

"Why—that's a perfect roundabout—with
its own lovely humming music too!"

"Yes. That's what I thought," said Betty,
pleased. "Do you think you could use it for
a roundabout at your Fair till the witch's
spell has worn off your own?"

"Yes—certainly I could!" said Heyho.
"But how could I spin it to make it go

round? I'm not big or strong enough."

"I'll put a Spin Spell into it," said Run-About. "Then it will spin itself whenever you say 'Spin, top, spin!'"

"Oh—thank you very much," said Heyho, delighted. "Can we take it now? How can we get it to the Fair?"

"We could take it in the wooden engine," said Robin. "In the second truck. Come on—let's all go. I'll have a ride on the Humming-Top Roundabout too!"

"I say! What fun!" said Betty, thrilled. "Can we do anything else, Mr. Heyho?"

"You can do anything you like," said Heyho, so happy that he was full of smiles. "You can go on the swings and down the slippery-slip and throw hoopla rings to see if you can get a prize, and have a go at the coconut shy, and . . ."

"Oh quick, I can't wait! Do come along!" cried Betty. "Where's the engine? Engine, we're off to Fairyland again!"

And soon away they went as usual, carrying the big top in the second truck. Betty stood in the first truck, as soon as she had been made small enough, and held the top steady, because it rolled round and round in the truck, and she was afraid it might be bumped out, and lost down the rabbit-hole.

It didn't take them very long to arrive at the Fair. It really was a fine one! There was a row of swings that went to and fro and up and down. There was a long and winding slippery-slip packed with squealing pixies. There was a coconut shy where many brownies were throwing balls at rows of coconuts standing on pegs.

And there was the roundabout, of course, but it stood still and silent. No music came from it, and no movement. All round it stood the little folk, looking very sad because

"A penny a spin! Only a penny!"

they couldn't have a ride on the lovely roundabout.

A man came stamping up, looking very cross. It was the owner of the Fair, Mr. Stamp-Around.

"Hey, there!" he called. "You've got to remove that roundabout. I want to put something else there. It's no use at all, that roundabout of yours, Heyho."

"I've found the very newest kind of roundabout there is!" shouted back Heyho. "It makes its own music—and sounds like a hundred bees!"

He and Run-About stood the great humming-top on its foot. Run-About rubbed a powerful spell all round it.

> "Now begin
> To spin, top, spin,
> Go round and round,
> With humming sound,
> And tumble people on the ground!"

The children heard him whispering this rhyme as he rubbed his magic on to the top. A low humming sound began to come from it.

"Climb up and hold on! The new roundabout is about to spin!" cried Heyho "A penny a spin! Only a penny!"

Soon the top was crowded with dozens of little folk, all laughing and chattering. What a queer roundabout!

"Spin, top, spin!" said Heyho—and at once the great top began to spin round and round, slowly at first, and then faster and faster! It hummed louder still, and an old woman nearby looked round and about, expecting to see a swarm of bees. But it was only the top humming!

What fun it was! And when the top slowed down, sending all the little folk rolling on the ground, how they laughed and shouted.

"It's a grand roundabout!" they said. "Let's go on it again!"

But this time Betty, Robin and Run-About were the only ones allowed on. How Betty squealed when the top went faster and faster, and filled her ears with its humming!

They all enjoyed it very much, and tumbled off happily when the top slowed down and rolled over. "Now let's try the other things!" said Robin.

And off they went to swing on the swings, and slide down the winding slippery-slip, and shy the wooden balls at the coconuts. Robin won a big one, and so did Run-About. Betty threw a hoop at the hoopla stall, and it fell exactly round a lovely little brooch. The hoopla man pinned it on her dress. She was so pleased.

They didn't want to leave the exciting Fair but they dared not be late for their dinner. What would they say if Mummy asked them where they had been that morning? She would never believe them if they told her that they had taken their hummingtop to a Fair and made it into a roundabout!

"You are a most exciting friend to have, Run-About," said Robin, as they went back in the little wooden train. "I do wonder what will happen next?"

FOR two days nothing happened at all, and the children were quite disappointed. Then somebody came to see Run-About, someone who looked most upset.

It was a pretty little pixie looking rather like the fairy doll who always stood at the top of the children's tree each Christmas. Run-About knew her at once, when she flew down into the playroom, where he was watching the children build with bricks.

He jumped up quickly. "Oh—Tiptoe! What's the matter? You're crying!"

The children looked at the pretty little thing and wished their hankies were small enough to wipe her eyes. She rubbed away her tears and tried to smile.

"Oh, Run-About—I'm sorry, to burst in like this, but it's very, very urgent."

"Tell me," said Run-About. "Nothing has happened to your sisters, has it?"

"Yes. Something dreadful!" said Tiptoe. "I was out shopping to-day when the Enchanter Frown-Hard came along to our cottage and saw my sisters playing in the garden. And he's captured them all and taken them away!"

"How shocking!" said Run-About, in dismay. "They'll be so frightened. Where has he taken them?"

"To the tower that reaches the clouds," said Tiptoe. "You know the one, don't you —its tip goes right up to the highest clouds. And he's going to keep them prisoners there just because the ball they were playing with hit him on his horrid long nose!"

"We must rescue them," said Run-About at once.

"But how, dear Run-About?" said Tiptoe. "We can't get into the tower, because he has taken the door away by magic—it's just brick wall all round."

"I'll put another one there," said Heyho, valiantly.

"But listen—after Frown-Hard had sent them all up to the very top of the tower, he made the *stairs* disappear too," said Tiptoe, beginning to cry again. "So it's just no good trying to get into the tower."

"The aeroplane!" suddenly said Betty. "Couldn't we fly to the top of the tower in that and rescue them?"

"No. The Enchanter thought of that," said Tiptoe, sadly. "He's got someone watching out for aeroplanes. He's already caught one, with my uncle in it. Oh dear— what are we to do?"

"Perhaps he wouldn't see an aeroplane at *night*?" said Betty. "Could we go then, do you think?"

"No. He'd hear it," said Tiptoe. Then she suddenly smiled. "Oh! *I* know! I know something that would fly to the top of the tower without a sound!"

"Who? What?" cried Run-About, excited.

"A kite!" said Tiptoe. "A kite on a very long string. Have these children got a kite? Oh, do say yes!"

They had, of course, and they at once went to their toy cupboard to find it. They pulled it out—a big flat kite with a smiling face and a long tail made of newspaper screwed up into pieces.

"Here it is," said Betty, pleased. "But Run-About, you mustn't make this kite smail when you get to Fairyland, or it would never take all Tiptoe's sisters! And how are they to come down on it? They would tumble off."

"Easy," said Run-About, "the kite must fly higher than the tower, and flap its long tail against the top window. Then each little sister can climb out and hang on to a bit of the tail! Then off the kite flies to our land!"

"Oh *yes*!" said Tiptoe. "Let's send a bee to hum the news to my sisters. The Enchanter would never notice such a small creature at the top of the tower!"

"We must wait till the evening," said Run-About. "It's no good flying a kite in the daytime—it would certainly be seen."

It was hard to wait so long, and Tiptoe sighed all day, thinking of her small scared sisters. They sent a message by a big bumble-bee and he came back to say that he had told the little pixies the news, and they would be sure to look out for the kite that night.

Once more the children and Run-About set off in the wooden engine. It was difficult to take the big kite down the rabbit-hole, so Run-About went a different way. He took them through a cave in a distant hill—and hey presto, when they came out of the big tunnel in the hill, they found themselves not far from the Meccano bridge that they

The Enchanter's Castle

had built over the river.

"It's still there!" said Robin, in delight. "Let's drive over it in the engine."

So they trundled over the bridge they had built, and it didn't even shake! Then on they went till they came to the Enchanter's castle, gleaming in the moonlight.

Some distance away was the high tower, soaring right up to the clouds. Goodness, how tall it was! But the kite wouldn't mind that—it liked flying high!

Run-About had a very big ball of string. He would need a lot if the kite was to fly as high as the clouds!

The wind blew a little and the kite tried to get out of the truck. "All right—be patient—you're soon going to fly!" said Run-About. "We'd better be very, very quiet now, everyone!"

The kite was taken from the truck. It

seemed very big to the children now, because, as usual, they had gone small as soon as they got into the train. It took all four of them to pull the kite into position so that the wind could take it.

"We'd better all of us hang on to the string," said Run-About. "My word—there it goes up into the air. Fly to the topmost window of the tower, kite—that's right—higher and higher—you're nearly there!"

THE kite rose high in the wind, and tugged so hard at the string that the children and Run-About were almost jerked off their feet. Little Tiptoe was pulled a few feet into the air, but Betty just dragged her down in time!

The string ran quickly through their fingers as the kite rose higher and higher, and nobody dared to hold it back now. Was the kite at the topmost window yet?

Yes, it was! It had reached the clouds, and its long paper tail tapped against the topmost tower window. Someone opened it cautiously.

Then, one by one, seven tiny little people climbed out, holding to the tail of the kite. The first one sat down on the first bit of paper, the next one sat down on the second, and so on.

"Hold tight to the string of the tail," whispered the first little sister. "Hold tight!"

Down below Tiptoe was waiting anxiously. She was too far away to see her sisters creeping out of the tower window—but the

four down below felt each little bump as the
seven sisters sat themselves on the bits of
paper that made the kite's tail.

"One — two — three — four — five — six —
seven—they're all out of the window now,
safely on the kite's tail!" said Tiptoe. "Pull
the kite down! Then we'll have them down
here with us in no time, and can escape in
the wooden train!"

But oh dear, oh dear, who should come
up behind them just at that very moment
but the horrid old Enchanter!

"Aha!" he said. "I've been watching
your clever little trick. But it won't do, you
know. I'll help you to pull down the kite—
and I'll capture those seven little sisters
again as soon as the kite reaches the ground.
And I'll have Tiptoe as well this time!"

What a dreadful shock for everyone! But
Run-About was not going to have the little
pixie sisters caught again. He whipped out
his knife and cut the string of the kite. At
once it soared high into the air, and flew off
all by itself into the sky—and it took the
seven little sisters with it, hanging on its tail!

"Quick, quick! Into the train!" cried Run-
About, and they all leapt in. The Enchanter
was so surprised by the disappearance of

the kite that he didn't even try to stop them!

Off they went through the night at top speed and didn't stop till they came into the garden again. Tiptoe was crying.

"I know my sisters have escaped from the Enchanter—but I'm sure I shall never see them again!" she sobbed.

"Don't be silly," said Run-About. "I rubbed a Come-Back spell on the kite before I sent it up into the air. You surely might have guessed that, Tiptoe."

"Well, I didn't," said Tiptoe. "Oh, how clever you are, Run-About. When will the kite come back?"

"I've no idea," said Run-About. "All I know is that it *will* come back, and will bring your sisters with it."

He took Tiptoe into the playroom with him, and she got into one of the dolls' cots with a doll, though she was sure she wouldn't go to sleep! Run-About went to the dolls' house and cuddled down into bed, quite tired out.

The children went to bed too, and when Betty heard a leaf tap-tapping against her window, she quite thought it was the kite, and got up to see.

But it wasn't! It hadn't come back the next

In an old blackbird's nest, fast asleep!

morning either, and Run-About felt quite
worried. Tiptoe cried and cried, and Betty
gave her two tiny hankies belonging to her
dolls.

They had to go out for a walk that morning, though they didn't want to leave Run-
About and Tiptoe. But Mummy said it was
lovely and fine, and the wind was very fresh,
and they really must go out!

And will you believe it, just as they crossed
the field that led to the farm, they saw a kite
tangled in a tree! Was it theirs? Could it be?

Yes—it was! How wonderful! Where were
the tiny sisters? Were they hurt?

They ran to the tree and climbed up. Yes, it *was* their kite, its string wrapped round and round some twigs. It really was a business to untie it! But where in the world were Tiptoe's sisters?

Betty suddenly saw them! They were all cuddled in an old blackbird's nest, fast asleep! How sweet they looked!

"There they are—tired out!" said Betty. "Robin, can you take the nest gently out of its place? We could carry all the little things quite safely home in the nest!"

Robin removed the old nest gently, and carried home the sleeping pixies. Betty took the kite. "The Come-Back spell can't have been quite strong enough!" she said. "You *nearly* got home, kite, but not quite!"

How pleased Run-About and Tiptoe were to see the seven little sisters asleep in the nest! Run-About couldn't help laughing out loud —and that woke them up!

The children loved them. They were as frisky and lively as kittens, and did the maddest things. Tiptoe decided that for one night they would all stay in the dolls' house before they went back home.

And you should have seen those tiny creatures running in and out of the front door, opening and shutting the windows, cooking on the little stove, and sitting on the little chairs!

But best of all was when Betty looked through the windows at night and saw them all cuddled into the little beds, fast asleep. I wish *we* could have seen them too, don't you?

THE children felt quite sad when Tip-toe and her seven tiny sisters went home together. Run-About took them in the little wooden train, and Robin and Betty wished they could go with them, but their Granny was coming to see them that day, so they couldn't.

"You'll come back, won't you, Run-About?" said Betty, anxiously, when he got into the cab of the engine. He nodded gaily.

"Oh yes—I haven't finished my holiday with you yet! I feel much better already. I love your dolls' house, it's just right for me!"

Off they went, and the children watched them go through the gap in the hedge. "They'll be going down the rabbit-hole now," said Betty. "My word—wouldn't other children love to know that there are secret ways into Fairyland all over the place —if you know where to look for them!"

"We know two already," said Robin. "The one down the rabbit-hole and the one through the cave in the hill."

"Of course, some of the entrances to

Fairyland are too small for us to use, unless we're lucky enough to know someone like Run-About, who knows a Go-Small spell," said Betty. "Look—there's Granny already!"

They ran to meet their Granny, and had a lovely day with her—but all the time they were listening for Run-About to come back. They had become very fond of the green-eyed brownie, with his long, silky beard and happy ways.

He didn't come back to dinner and he didn't come back to tea, because they looked in the dolls' house to see. The wooden engine wasn't back either.

"I expect he's spending the day with Tip-toe and her sisters," said Robin. "They really are very sweet!"

Even when bedtime came near Run-About wasn't back. The children felt sad. "We can't possibly go and see him," said Robin, mournfully. "We don't know the Go-Small spell, and if we tried to find the way through that cave in the hill by ourselves, we might lose ourselves."

"Listen—there's an owl hooting outside," said Betty, suddenly. "He sounds as if he's very close. Could he be bringing a message for us, do you think?"

In his beak was a scrap of paper

Robin went to the window. A large owl sat on a branch outside, his big eyes gleaming as he waited. In his sharp curved beak was a scrap of paper. He dropped it when he saw the children, spread his soft wings and flew off silently.

"Yes—it *is* a message!" said Robin, excited. "Oh goodness me—Granny has spotted it too. She's picking it up and reading it!"

He ran down the stairs, and Granny came in from the garden at the same time, holding the scrap of paper. She held it out to Robin.

"I was just walking round the garden in

the evening sunshine, when this note dropped at my feet," she said, sounding puzzled. "Is it for you? It must be from one of your friends, though where it came from I really don't know. Perhaps the wind brought it!"

Robin took the note and read it. "Yes, Granny," he said, "it *is* from one of our friends. Thank you. I'll just go and tell Betty."

Off he went, and he and Betty read the note together. It was from Run-About.

"Shall not be home to-night, as Tiptoe is giving a tea-party at midnight to her aunt, Lady High-and-Mighty, who is passing through her village. She is half a witch, and rides on a very fine broomstick with a handle made of gold, and bristles of pure silk! I wish you could come to the party too, but Tiptoe only has ten cups and saucers— that will be seven for her sisters, and one each for herself and for me and for her aunt! She sends her love. See you to-morrow.

"Your friend, Run-About."

"Oh! I do *wish* we could go to the party too!" said Betty. "A midnight party in

Fairyland, with Tiptoe and her sisters—
and a guest who is half a witch."

"She'll come riding down on her golden
broomstick!" said Robin. "Listen—there's
Mummy calling. We'd better get ready for
bed at once!"

They were soon asleep—but, just about
half-past eleven there came a rattling up the
garden path. Robin heard it in his sleep,
and awoke suddenly. He knew that rattling
noise! It was the sound
made by the wheels of the
little wooden train. Run-
About must be back!

He sat up in bed, and
soon heard the patter of
tiny feet in his bedroom.
"Robin! Are you awake?"
said Run-About's voice.
"I want your help. Some-
thing dreadful has hap-
pened!"

"What?" asked Robin.

"Well, you know that
Tiptoe was giving a mid-
night party for her aunt,
don't you? She had just set

"Everything smashed" the table with all the cups

and saucers and plates, when suddenly one leg of the table collapsed—and everything fell to the floor and was smashed!"

"Oh dear—what a pity!" said Robin.

"Yes—because there are no shops open to buy another tea-set," said Run-About. "So I wondered if Betty would lend us her lovely dolls' tea-set, Robin—it's got twelve cups and saucers and plates, hasn't it?"

"Oh yes! Betty would love to lend it to Tiptoe for her party!" said Robin. "Let's go and tell her."

"And, as there are *twelve* cups and saucers, would you and Betty like to come to the party too?" said Run-About as they went into Betty's room. "Tiptoe only had ten, so she couldn't ask you—but if we have twelve, you could come too. Please do!"

"We'll come! We'll *love* to come!" said Robin in excitement. "Oh, *what* an adventure!"

BETTY was just as excited as Robin was, when she was awakened and told the news. She scrambled out of bed at once.

"I'll get the tea-set now. What a good thing nothing is broken—there are twelve of everything still, and a lovely teapot and milk-jug and sugar-basin. Oh, I *never* thought we could use it properly, like this! What fun to be as small as you, Run-About, and drink from my own tiny tea-set!"

"Come in your dressing-gowns," said Run-About. "There won't be time for you to dress."

Betty got her tea-set out of the toy cupboard, in its big box. She took the lid off and peeped inside. How tiny the cups were —but soon they would be big enough for her to drink from, because she would be as small as a doll!

Down the stairs—into the garden where the wooden train waited. Once more they became as small as Run-About and climbed into the trucks. Betty still felt as if she were going down in a lift, when the Go-Small spell worked!

Off they went at top speed, almost running over a startled hedgehog, and making two little mice squeak in fright. Down the rabbit-hole, hoping not to bump into any running rabbit, and at last out of the other end and into Fairyland itself!

"Oh! Isn't Fairyland beautiful to-night, with the moon shining down brightly?" said Betty. "And look—that tree is bright with candles! It's like a Christmas tree. Who put the candles on it, Run-About?"

"Nobody. It *grows* candles!" said Run-About. "If we had time to stop you could pick some. But we really must hurry. Tiptoe's aunt doesn't like to be kept waiting. I only hope she's late!"

They came to Tiptoe's cottage. She had hung it with fairy-lights and it looked very pretty indeed. Roses and honeysuckle grew all over it, right to the crooked little chimney, and scented the air as soon as they came near.

Tiptoe was waiting at the gate. She ran to meet them, her eyes shining. "Oh, I'm so glad you've come! And you've brought the tea-set Run-Around told me of—oh, isn't it lovely! Just the right size too. We'll soon have the table laid again!"

The seven little sisters twittered round the children like small birds. It was queer to be as small now as they were!

Soon they were laying the table in Tiptoe's cottage, and the two children gazed in astonishment—for there was not a scrap of food there, but only empty dishes. Well, well, well!

"Here's our Aunt High-and-Mighty!" said Tiptoe, suddenly, running into the garden. Robin and Betty went too. What a strange sight they saw!

A shining golden broomstick was flying high above their heads in the moonlight, and on it rode somebody in a pointed hat and a long and beautiful red cloak that flew out behind in the wind. She pointed the broomstick downwards and swooped towards the garden.

She leapt off the shining broomstick and stood it against the wall. The children stared at her curiously. So this was Tiptoe's aunt, half a witch!

She smiled round and her green eyes twinkled. "Ha! Quite a party!" she said. "I hope you've got a meal for me, Tiptoe.

Somebody in a pointed hat and red cloak

I've flown right across Fairyland to-night and I'm hungry."

"Come in, Aunt," said Tiptoe. "This is Run-About the brownie—and this is Robin and Betty, two good friends of ours. Your midnight tea is ready!"

They all went into the cottage. There were not enough chairs to go round the table, so Tiptoe had put two benches at each side, and a chair at each end, one for herself and one for her aunt.

They all sat down. "Why isn't there anything to eat?" said Robin, puzzled.

Everyone laughed except Betty. "This

is a special meal," said Tiptoe. "My aunt once gave me a spell for parties, and I'm using it to-night. We each wish for what we want to eat, and the empty dishes will soon be filled!"

"What a splendid idea!" said Betty, excited. It certainly was fun when they all wished one by one!

"Dewdrop cake!" said Aunt High-and-Mighty. "Honey buns!" said Run-About. "Treacle pudding!" said Robin. "Chocolate ice-cream!" said Betty. "Mystery sandwiches!" said Tiptoe, and all the seven sisters wished for curious and exciting things too!

A dish was filled by magic each time anyone wished. It really was very peculiar, but the children thought that it was quite the nicest way of getting food for a party. How they enjoyed their midnight meal!

Aunt High-and-Mighty was a most interesting person. Tiptoe said she knew a great deal of magic and had done some extraordinary things. "Please, aunt, do tell us a few!" she said.

So the honoured guest told some very strange and mysterious tales, and the children almost stopped eating when they heard them. How they wished that, like Tiptoe, they had an aunt who was half a witch!

Tiptoe's aunt said goodbye at last, and went to get her broomstick. She suddenly turned to the two children. "I like you," she said. "You're nice children with good manners. Would you like me to take you home on my broomstick, just for a treat? Jump on, then—that's right. Hold tight, we're off!"

There they go, up in the air on the shining broomstick—*what* a thing to happen!

THE children sat on the broomstick handle, holding tight with their hands, too excited for words as they flew through the moonlit night. Tiptoe's aunt hummed a little magic song as they went along, and the children suddenly felt sleepy.

"Oh—I'm falling asleep—and I shall fall off the broomstick!" said Betty. "Please, please stop!"

"I'm falling asleep too," said Robin, in alarm, and he gave an enormous yawn. "Please, Tiptoe's aunt, fly down to earth. I know I shall fall off!"

But Tiptoe's aunt took no notice and went on humming more and more loudly. The children's eyes closed. They let go the broomstick—they felt themselves falling, falling, falling—then BUMP! They arrived somewhere soft and bounced up and down.

"Goodness!" said Robin, only half awake even now, "where am I? On my bed, I do believe. But—but how did it happen!"

Betty had landed on her bed too, but she

was too sleepy to think about it. In two seconds both the children were sound asleep, still hearing the humming noise in their dreams.

They were puzzled next day about how they fell into their beds, and even Run-About, who had arrived back in the wooden train, couldn't tell them. "Tiptoe's aunt knows a lot of very powerful magic," he said. "I wouldn't worry about how you got back to your beds, your right size, too, if I were you! You were very lucky to have a broomstick ride, I can tell you! I've never had one in my life!"

"We did enjoy ourselves," said Betty, remembering the wonderful meal. "Oh, Run-About—I wish you knew the spell to make food-wishes

Falling, falling . . .

come true! It would be such fun to have
a party like that, and let each of our guests
wish for exactly what they liked!"

"I enjoyed those Mystery sandwiches,"
said Robin. "I couldn't guess what was
inside any of them, but each one was nicer
than the last. I wish I had a few to eat
now."

Run-About grinned, and took them to the
dolls' house. Inside, on the table, was a little
paper bag. He took it and went out to offer
it to them. Inside were some of the Mystery
sandwiches, left over from the party—but
they were very, very small, of course.

"I know enough magic to make them big
enough for you to eat, if you like," he said.
"Tiptoe sent them to you."

"Oh! How lovely!" said Robin. "Please
do make them big now—as big as you
can!"

Soon they were eating the Mystery sandwiches, and puzzling their heads to try and
think what was inside them.

"Sardines — egg — tomato — cream —
chocolate—pineapple—peppermint—goodness, I can taste all those at once!" said
Betty.

"We *have* enjoyed ourselves since you

came to live with us, Run-About," said
Robin. "Life has really been very exciting.
I do hope you won't go away yet."

"I really must go next week," said Run-
About. "It's been a lovely holiday, I must
say—though I've had to do quite a lot of
jobs, haven't I—with your help, of course."

"We've *loved* helping!" said Betty. "It
was lucky we had so many toys that were just
what you wanted—the Meccano for the
bridge—and the tea-set last night . . ."

"And the kite for rescuing Tiptoe's sisters
from the tower," said Robin. "And the

Soon they were eating the Mystery sandwiches

humming-top came in well for that round-about."

"And the aeroplane!" said Run-About. "And don't forget how useful your dolls' house has been to me. I've used it for a proper little holiday-house! I shall be sorry to leave it next week."

"I hope something else happens before you go back to live in Fairyland," said Betty. "Things will be *very* dull without you, Run-About!"

"I don't expect anything will," said Run-About. "There's nothing much on in Fairy-land at present, except the balloon-racing on Friday."

"Balloon-racing! What's that?" said Robin, surprised.

"Oh, it's rather amusing," said Run-About. "You know those lovely balloons that you can blow up? Well, we enter those for the race."

"But—what happens? Do you just blow about?" asked Betty.

"Well, when they're blown up nice and big, we fix a little basket under each one, and the racers each get into them," said Run-About. "Then they all set off at a given moment, and see who can go the farthest before the balloon goes flat, or drifts to earth."

"It sounds wonderful!" said Robin. "You do do exciting things, Run-About. Are *you* going in for the balloon-race?"

"Rather!" said Run-About. "I nearly won it last year. I got a friendly breeze to puff me very hard."

"Can *we* go and see the race?" said Betty. "Say yes, Run-About! What time will it be?"

"It's in the afternoon," said the little brownie.

"We could come!" said Betty. "Mother's going to see Granny then, and she's not going to take us. We could come!"

"All right. I'll fetch you," said Run-About. "But you'll have to look after yourselves, because I shall be up in my balloon. Perhaps you'll bring me luck!"

BETTY and Robin could hardly wait till Friday. They looked out some of the old balloons they had had at their last party and blew them up.

"We'll have a little balloon-race ourselves in the garden!" said Betty. "You take the two red ones, Robin, I'll have the blue ones. We'll throw them up into the wind and see whose balloons reach the other end of the garden first!"

The wind took the balloons along fast, bouncing and bumping them through the air. Betty's blue one won.

"It won because I had blown it up so big," she said. "That's why it won!"

They asked Run-About what colour balloon he was going to race in.

"Yellow," he said. "I've got it put away carefully at home. We'll get it on our way to the races."

When Friday came the children rushed off with Run-About in the little wooden train. They trundled through Fairyland till they came to Run-About's little cottage. There were still no doors to be seen, but Run-About soon altered that!

Just as he had done before, he pencilled a little door in the wall, and hey presto, it was a real door! He knocked and went in.

"Why do you knock?" said Robin.

"Just to see if I'm at home!" said Run-About, and that made the children giggle. He went to a chest and opened the lid. Inside lay a big piece of wrinkled-up yellow rubber—his balloon! He took it out and tucked it under his arm.

"I'm glad I remembered where I put it!" he said. "Come along—we mustn't be late."

Out they went, and he slammed the door. It vanished at once. *What* a fine way of making sure that no burglars could get in!

Off they went again in the wooden train and soon came to the field where the balloon-races were to be held. There were hundreds of little folk there, all very excited.

Run-About went to the starting-point, and shook out his yellow rubber balloon. "Are you going to blow it up?" asked Robin. "You will need a lot of breath!"

"Oh—I just pop a Blow-Up spell into the neck of the balloon," said Run-About. "Look!"

He popped a tiny blue pellet into the neck of the balloon and blew on it. At once there came a hissing sound and the balloon began to fill with air!

"I wish I had a spell like that when we give a party and I have to blow up all the balloons," said Robin. "You really do have such good ideas in Fairyland!"

Run-About turned to watch someone else's balloon being blown up by a spell. His own grew bigger and bigger and bigger—simply enormous! Betty watched it in admiration. How much bigger would it go? Surely it would burst if it grew much bigger?

"Run-About—don't you think you ought to stop your Blow-Up spell now?" she called. Run-About swung round to look at his balloon, and he gave a shout.

"My goodness—it'll burst. Stop, Blow-Up spell!"

But he was just too late. The balloon was almost as big as a cottage! It wobbled a little —and then burst with a most tremendous BANG! Everybody fell down flat. The balloon disappeared completely except for a few bits of yellow rubber flying through the air.

Run-About sat up, and tears came into his eyes.

"My beautiful balloon! Why didn't I watch it carefully? Now I can't go in for the race. It was my only balloon."

Everybody fell down flat

"Oh Run-About—I *am* sorry!" said Betty. "Can't you buy one anywhere?"

Robin suddenly put his hand in his pocket. He had remembered that he had stuffed his and Betty's balloons there, when he had let the air out of them after their little garden race.

"Run-About—have one of mine!" he called, excitedly. "Look, take this blue one, it blows up nice and big!"

Run-About came over to him in excitement. "My word—do you mean to say you actually brought your own balloons in your pocket! What a bit of luck. Yes, I'd like that blue one, please—you told me how well it blew away in the wind!"

He pushed a little Blow-Up spell into the balloon's neck, and then blew on it. The children watched it slowly swell up, bigger and bigger and bigger!

"Watch it, watch it!" said Robin. "Its skin is looking thin now. It may burst!"

But it didn't! Run-About stopped the Blow-Up spell at exactly the right moment.

He ran to get the little baskets that each racing balloonist had to tie underneath with rope. He soon attached his and got into it at the starting-line.

All the racers had to hold tightly to a piece of rope stretched across the field, or their balloons would have gone up into the air at once, the wind was so strong!

"One—two—three—GO!" shouted a

voice, and every racer let go the starting-rope.

"Good luck, Run-About, good luck!" shouted the children. "We do hope you'll fly farther than anyone else. Good luck!"

Run-About's balloon had shot high into the air and the wind took it nicely. Would it win the race? Mind that holly-bush, Run-About! Fly, balloon, fly fast!

THERE came a little rattling noise beside the children, and Robin looked round. It was the wooden engine!

"Oh Betty—the engine wants us to get in so that we can follow the balloons!" said Robin. So in they both got and the little train rattled away over the countryside after the balloons. There were altogether twelve in the race.

Pop! One blew against a pine-tree and the pine needles pricked it! Bang! Another blew against a tall holly-tree and that was the end of that.

A third one began to go down flat, and then two more. "Only seven left now, and Run-About is second," said Robin, looking up from the little train.

Bang! Bang! Two more burst. That left five. Then one drifted right down to the ground instead of flying. That left four.

Bang! Oh, dear, was that Run-About's? No, it was another blue balloon that had gone pop. Only three left—and look, one was gradually going down, smaller and smaller.

Ah, that was out of the race too.

Now only Run-About's blue balloon was left and a big green one. Run-About was second, but soon a little wind found him and blew him into first place.

The wooden train rattled on, following the two balloons, and behind it came all kinds of coaches and cars carrying little folk who meant to see the finish!

"Oh! Run-About's balloon is beginning to go down—it's getting smaller!" cried Betty, in dismay. She was right—it was already much smaller! Oh, dear!

"The *green* balloon's going down now, too!" shouted someone behind. So it was. What an excitement!

The green balloon kept valiantly up to the blue one, though each was now getting very much smaller, and was drifting down towards the ground. The green one got caught in a bush, and before it could get free Run-About's balloon had gone a good way ahead. But it was going down very fast now, and was a very tiny little thing!

The green balloon sailed on again. The blue one came down to earth, quite flat, and lay there as if it were tired out. Everyone began to shout.

"The green one will win! It's almost up to the blue one. It's winning!"

But no—just a few yards behind Run-About's blue balloon the green one collapsed and dropped down to the grass. It couldn't float even a yard further.

"Run-About's won! The blue balloon has won!" shouted everyone. "It got farther than the green one! Hurrah for Run-About, he's won at last!"

Run-About looked very pleased indeed. He came over to Robin and Betty. "It was all because of you and your fine balloon!"

Run-About's balloon had gone ahead

he said. "I wouldn't have won in my yellow one, I'm sure. Thank you very much!"

"What's the prize?" asked Robin, as they trundled back to the starting-point in the little wooden train.

"It's a Magic Sweet-Bag," said Run-About.

"Whatever's that?" asked Betty.

"Just a little paper bag of sweets, which is never empty, however many you eat," said Run-About.

"What a wonderful prize!" said Robin. "A sweet-bag that is always full of sweets!"

"Yes—you can wish for any kind you like," said Run-About. "Ah—here we are!"

Everyone clapped Run-About as he went to receive the prize. He came straight back to the children. He held out the sweet-bag, which looked nice and full.

"Here you are!" he said. "It's for you! You have helped me such a lot while I've stayed in your playroom, and I want you to have this as a little gift from me! You'll love it."

"Oh, THANK you, Run-About!" said the children, hardly believing their ears. A magic sweet-bag was never empty—why, there couldn't be a more wonderful present than that!

It certainly was marvellous. The children enjoyed it very much indeed for the next few days. It didn't matter what they wished for—chocolates, toffees, peppermints, fudge —the bag was always full of whatever sweets they wanted!

It was sad to say goodbye to Run-About when his holiday came to an end. He cleaned up the dolls' house nicely before he went, and polished the wooden train.

"Please, PLEASE come and see us whenever you can!" begged Betty. "We shall miss you dreadfully. When shall we see you again, Run-About?"

"It's my birthday soon, so you must come to my party," said the little brownie, his green eyes twinkling at them. "I'll send you an invitation. You'll see me often. If ever I want to borrow any of your toys, I'll come and ask you."

"Please do!" said Robin. "And if we want to see you *very* badly, we'll somehow find a way into Fairyland."

"I'm going now," said Run-About. "Goodbye—and thank you for all you've done for me. I've loved it."

"Take the wooden engine to get back in," said Robin. Run-About shook his head.

"No. I'll walk down the rabbit-hole, thank you. It's not really very far."

Off he went, and the two children were sad to see him go. What a wonderful time they had had with him—and what a good thing they had had so many toys they could lend him!

Betty looked as if she were going to cry. But Robin knew how to stop that! He took up the Magic Sweet-Bag and opened it.

"Have a sweet!" he said. "Cheer up, Betty—we're going to the birthday party— we know the way to Fairyland—and we've got a Magic Sweet-Bag! We're very, very lucky!"

So they are! Don't you think so?